Protected

Tropic Storm, Volume 1

Kira Parke

Published by Kira Parke, 2018.

This is a work of fiction. Similarities to real people, places, or events are entirely coincidental.

PROTECTED

First edition. December 5, 2018.

ISBN: 979-8230496021

Written by Kira Parke.

For everyone who ever needed an escape.

Chapter One

An Undiscovered Country

Lydia Hawkins loved takeoffs, but hated landings. Takeoffs were so hopeful and landings seemed anticlimactic. To her, landing felt like an ending, not a beginning. As she braced herself for the dreaded impact of wheels to tarmac, Lydia felt an ominous shudder shoot up her spine. Her long plane journey had come to an end, but a new path lay, sprawled ahead of her. This particular landing would be anything *but* anticlimactic. She pulled at her long, chestnut ponytail. Her black cap and sunglasses made her almost unrecognizable, if the image from her phone's selfie-camera was to be believed. Her faded blue jeans and long- sleeved blouse, ensured that barely an inch of skin was visible. She tugged at her sleeves, pulling them down past her wrists. Lydia examined her pale hands and they were trembling. She interlocked her fingers and wedged them between her knees.

A wave of clicking spread through the airplane, as impatient people relieved themselves of their seatbelts. Lydia wished for a moment that she could keep hers fastened until the aircraft took off again. She fantasized about travelling forever, although travelling coach for all eternity was plain unappealing. Lydia tried to picture herself in first-class, but couldn't. Who was she, anyway? Suddenly, the harsh crossfire of an argument cut through the cabin; something about luggage? Lydia tried to block out the disturbance, but found it impossible. The cutting words hacked their way into her head. To Lydia, it sounded like the cruel dissonance of a car crash. Lydia suddenly felt quite ill.

"You getting up, love?" enquired the elderly gentleman, sitting in the window seat beside Lydia.

"Guess I have to, huh?" she replied meekly.

"First time in Australia?" asked the man in a shaky, Australian drawl that made Lydia forget her jitters for a moment and smile.

"As a matter of fact, it is."

"Where is that lovely accent from?"

"I'm from the States. Colorado," said Lydia, instantly regretting being so candid with someone she didn't know.

"Well, you're going to have a rippa' of a time, blossom," said the older man with a wink.

"That's good, right?" questioned Lydia playfully.

The brief interaction with the stranger had provided Lydia with a needed distraction. It had muffled the chattering in her mind. She even found herself a little excited by the thought of her new life. Maybe she really could become someone different, given enough time. It wasn't too much to ask, was it? People had done similar things throughout history: disappearing from one world, only to reemerge across the sea, in a new one, for the purpose of building something better for themselves. Lydia had spent hours as a child, pawing over maps of the world, embarking on long journeys in her mind. Where had that little girl gone? The one who at five-years old, would stay up late, drawing lions, tigers and kangaroos by torchlight. Back then, she had thought that all of those animals lived together on the same island. She was so sick and tired of who she had become. Later in life, when things had taken a turn, Lydia learnt to smile along with other carefree twenty-somethings, but she was never really one of them. Now in her thirties, maybe it was her chance to start over. She stood up, smoothed out her sleeves and readied herself for the new world.

As Lydia rounded her way past the buxom, bubbly and very blonde flight attendant and exited the plane, she was greeted by thick, tropical warmth. It reminded Lydia of sinking below the surface of a hot bath. There was a floral scent in the air, accompanied by something that Lydia couldn't quite put a finger on. The sunlight was more brilliant and golden than any she had encountered before. Despite the shimmering heat, she could see brooding, storm-cloud laden mountains, off in the distance, as she walked the path to the terminal. Lydia tried her best to commit the landscape to memory. Perhaps she would buy some paints later on; she hadn't painted anything in such a long time. There was something dreamy and intoxicating about the place, but Lydia was quick to snap herself back to reality; she'd have to keep her wits about her.

'Welcome to Coolangatta Airport', read the brightly colored sign overhead. Lydia dragged her wheeled suitcase toward the main exit and tried to remember how to pronounce the name of the locale. She couldn't remember quite how the plane's Captain had said it when they were coming in to land. There was a lot about this country she was yet to learn; it cemented just how far from home she now was. Suddenly, she felt her stomach churning and nausea came at Lydia in waves. She bolted across the terminal to the bathroom and burst into the only empty cubicle, before vomiting convulsively.

As she washed her face, too spent to really notice the looks from others, Lydia realized that she wasn't tied up in knots over being so far from home. Sure, she was sad to leave behind her mom, her sister, her job and of course, her friends. She had changed her mind about leaving her life behind, at least a dozen times before buying the ticket. Lydia had felt unbridled anguish when the plane's landing gear had left the ground and the world she once knew, shrunk out of sight. But, no, it wasn't the thought of the eight thousand or so miles between her old home and what would soon be her new one. It wasn't the feeling that she was so far away; it was the fear that she wasn't far away enough.

Lydia walked through the automatic doors and interior cool surrendered to tropic humidity. People buzzed all around, busily kissing hello or goodbye. A teenaged boy with long, dark hair, strummed a guitar as a blonde girl in a midriff, sang something written before she was born. Then, a sudden streak of white, as a flock of birds zoomed overhead, screeching like they had just witnessed a crime. A spray-tanned man in a white, linen shirt, whizzed past Lydia, making kissy noises at her as he went. Lydia stared at her feet and released her grip on her case, so she could smooth out the sleeves of her top. She was about to seek out the sanctuary of the terminal once again, when her ears were accosted by a loud shriek.

"Yooooooooo hooooooo!" Lydia's nerves gave way to relief as she clapped eyes on a familiar face.

"You look like you could use a drink!" announced the culprit, jovially.

"Oh, it's you. I thought a fire alarm had gone off!" quipped Lydia. "It's great to see you, Dora." The pair embraced tightly, Dora wrapping her arms around Lydia's waist, as she was almost a foot shorter than her friend.

"This all you brought?" questioned Dora, as she deftly slipped from Lydia's grasp and grabbed hold of her luggage.

"Yeah. It was all pretty hasty," replied Lydia with a far-off look.

"Never mind, petal. New life: new wardrobe!" returned Dora, throwing the small case into the back of her tiny car.

"Thanks for coming, Dor," said Lydia breathlessly, stopping before opening the passenger door. "This is all just so..."

"I know, love. I know."

DORA WOVE THE LITTLE, aqua-blue hatchback through traffic like a racecar driver, but she spoke as calmly as someone riding the bus, "You're going to love my rental property, Lyds. I'm a bloody spectacular landlord too. I never interfere, I never nag about the rent. Well, I'll never nag you, cos' you're a good mate. You pay when you can and not before, my love. When we first met, in the states, I knew instantly that we were kindreds, you and me. Anyway, I had this other couple in, hippies from a place called Nimbin, down south a bit, I'll take you there one day if you like, but oh, my word, they were hopeless when it came to paying the rent..." rattled Dora.

Lydia half-listened, but she was distracted by the ocean; she could see it through the open, driver-side window, just past Dora's - very animated - face. She had never seen the sea up close and now here it was. The water was azure blue and the reflected sunlight shone, diamond-like, on its surface. Tall, pale buildings rose up on either side of the wide road; buildings with names like: 'Pacific Towers' and 'Ocean Paradise'. Dora was forced to slow down, as they plunged into mid-week traffic; it allowed Lydia the chance to watch people going to, or coming from the beach. The locals really stuck out, with their perma-tans and sun-bleached hair. The women looked as though they had been created in a test tube; each one more perfect than the last. Lydia tugged at her sleeves; it would have been intimidating, if she wasn't so intent on *not* being noticed. But would covering up make her stick out more? At any rate, she would limit her trips outdoors.

Dora pulled into the driveway of the old rental house, to the tune of much sputtering and backfiring. "Are you going to make it home?" asked Lydia with some concern.

"No worries! She always sounds like she's at death's door, pet, but Delilah has a lotta' heart for an old girl."

"You named your car Delilah?"

"Oh, she's a total minx," replied Dora with a cheeky wink.

Lydia looked up through the dusty windshield, "Why does this house have legs?" she enquired.

"It's a Queensland thing. Cos' of the, you know: flooding."

"Should I be worried?" asked Lydia, with more than a hint of trepidation.

"Nah! It hasn't flooded here in….days," said Dora, with a straight face.

Dora motioned a jangly, Bangle-laden arm for Lydia to exit the car and head inside. The warm air was tempered by a sea-breeze and there was a scent that Lydia guessed to be coconut husks; there were fallen coconuts all over the front yard. A good number of coconut palms had sprung up in random places around the front of the house, alongside what looked like avocado and papaya trees. The stairs up to the front porch creaked and there was a crooked fly-screen door, that fell languidly to the side when Lydia pulled it open. The main door was reassuringly solid and it opened to reveal a long hallway with rich, dark timber flooring. Lydia explored every corner and was happy to find that every room was tastefully furnished with beautifully maintained pieces from the nineteen-fifties.

The main bedroom featured a handsome, freshly polished, brass bed-frame, sporting a brand new, luxuriantly clothed mattress. There was a very fine, see-through curtain, draped over the bed from the ceiling.

"For the mozzies," remarked Dora, materializing behind Lydia.

"Mozzies?" Lydia queried.

"Mosquitoes. I forget that you're from a whole other country. Mozzie is Aussie for mosquito, pet," replied Dora.

"They're bad here?"

"They'll carry you away and make you their Queen," Dora said cryptically.

There was a fireplace in the main living room that Lydia figured she would never need in the Queensland climate. The mantle was painted a crisp white and it was adorned with large shells and other things from the ocean. There was a comfortable looking sofa setting and two large, cane chairs with lavish cushions. Lydia clicked with the kitschy charm of the place immediately; there was a sense of innocence, but something else, sadness maybe. Lydia daydreamed about the lives that had possibly intersected in the house over its long life.

There was also a feeling that some of those energies hadn't completely moved on.

"You can feel it, can't you?" enquired Dora, appearing in the doorway of the main bedroom like a specter.

"What am I feeling, exactly?" replied Lydia, her eyes squinting to see the unknown.

"The specialness of this house. I feel like...destiny awaits you here, love."

Lydia stared at Dora, silhouetted against the syrupy sunlight. She looked like a gypsy in her dangly, amethyst earrings and peasant skirt. Dora's flaming, Celtic red hair was kept off her triangular face with a patterned head-scarf. Her large, grey eyes were soulful and deep; her confident smile always seemed to say: 'I know things that you don't.'

"I'm gonna' let you unpack your comically tiny suitcase and get settled. I took the liberty of setting up a pre-paid phone for you, it's under my name and you don't have to worry about paying a bloody thing. I'll take care of it. I left my address written down for you on the fridge and you have my phone number if you need anything, okay my pet. There are some essentials for you in the kitchen and clean towels in the bathroom," said Dora warmly.

"Dora. Thank you so much. You're my only friend in the world right now."

"You just take care of yourself, Lyds. I'll pop over and check on you some time. I'll bring my home-made strawberry wine. You'll bloody love it. See you, petal."

Lydia felt a swell of love for Dora at that moment; they hadn't seen one another for a year at least and here she was, ready to help out a friend from the other side of the world, at a moment's notice. What would she have done without that kind of support? All the same, this was going to be a challenging chapter in Lydia's life and she would need to avoid thinking about the big picture for a while; things could get overwhelming, if not taken a bite at a time.

Lydia unpacked her clothes into a tall-boy in the bedroom, which only filled a drawer and a half. She perused the items in the pantry and, after finding some pots and pans hung up above the old stove, decided on a little pasta for dinner. A good dose of carbs always felt like a maternal hug in times of stress. As the water boiled, Lydia forced open a stubborn, wood-framed window, to let the steam out. A small bird, with a large head, plopped down on a branch of one of the gum trees in the yard below. It parted its beak and let out a loud, cackling sound that made Lydia jump.

"You must be a...Cook-a-burry? Lydia said dubiously, as she dropped dry spaghetti into bubbling water. "Mom would know how to say it."

Lydia's mom had read every book about Australia she could get her hands on. They'd talked about travelling to the 'land down-under' together, from the time Lydia was old enough to talk. Her mother would ambush Lydia with random facts about Australia, whenever she could: 'Did you know Australia is almost the same size as mainland America?' she would say, as Lydia's eyes widened in amazement. 'Did you know that Australia is home to twenty-one of the world's twenty-five most venomous snake species?'

Lydia gazed outside, at the blood-red sunset and tasted tears. She was crying for the first time in months. She had been so resolute about her escape plans, so laser-focused, that she hadn't allowed herself the indulgence of tears; now they all came in an almost overwhelming torrent. "Get it together!" Lydia chided herself. She drained the pasta and plated her food in a chipped bowl, not adding any embellishments to the plain noodles. Outside, a chorus of bullfrogs grew louder, under the cover of spreading darkness. Lydia sat at the dining room table, eating mechanically, staring into space. The house groaned and shifted, as though it were trying to get comfortable and Lydia was suddenly very aware that she was all alone. She picked up her phone and hesitated for a moment before sending her sister a text message. A reply came back almost immediately.

"Are U OK?"

"Yes. Everything's great. Is everything OK there?" asked Lydia.

"I miss U. So much," texted Kitty.

"Me 2. Love you."

"Love you more. Call me when you can, OK?

"I will. Stay safe. Talk soon," wrote Lydia.

Lydia wiped her damp face on her sleeve and sniffed hard. She shuffled over to a tiny television, atop a small, wooden table and turned it on. The news was on and it was a little jarring, hearing news-anchors speak in Australian accents, about things like sugar-cane prices and boats capsizing off the coast. Nevertheless, the warmth of the TV was comforting and it made the big, old house feel significantly homelier. The bullfrog choir's lullaby, with its steady rhythm, sang Lydia to sleep.

LYDIA'S HEAD JERKED back violently. She rolled her eyes around in their sockets, rousing herself from her unplanned catnap. Something wasn't quite right. Then there it was, the noise that had woken her: a rustling sound, that Lydia hoped she was imagining. There was something else, an absence of something: the bullfrogs had stopped croaking. She sat upright and a chill ran the length of her back, as she waited for the disruption to confirm itself. There was nothing forthcoming, for what seemed like an eternity and then, there it was again. It sounded like bushes being disturbed by something; maybe a dog? Hopefully a dog. Lydia tried to purge her thoughts of the images that appeared to her in that moment. She was terrified of facing up to her suspicions. Should she make a dash for the front door? No, that's what stupid bimbos in horror movies always did, right before the slasher stabbed them to death. The floor seemed to drop away and Lydia felt light-headed. Why did Dora leave her there alone?

Lydia summoned all her will and bolted upright. She tip-toed across to the open kitchen window and, closing her eyes, she counted to ten, then peered out. Her heart was pounding like a fist that threatened to punch its way out of her chest. Her eyes adjusted to the dark and, at first, she could see nothing, until a figure slowly took shape: a man. The intruder crouched, with his head down, so it was impossible to see his face, but Lydia felt the world spin, as all her fears come to light at once. He had finally found her, hadn't he? How did he track her down, so damned quickly? She shrunk back from the window and frantically pawed through the kitchen drawers, until she found a large, steak-knife.

Lydia felt as though she might faint, as the rustling moved along the rear of the house. When the stairs began to creak, Lydia's heart skipped a beat. Was the back door locked? Lydia snuck over to the door and just as she reached for the latch, the door-knob began to jiggle. Lydia gripped the handle of her knife tightly, as she braced herself. The back-door opened slowly and the intruder lurched inside, falling to the floor. Lydia's body coursed with adrenaline and she arced up, the knife clasped in both hands and raised above her head. "No! Wait!" the man protested huskily. Lydia stopped short of plunging the blade into the man's chest, when she saw the blood already pooling under his right shoulder.

Chapter Two

Stranger in a Strange Land

Lydia opened her mouth, but nothing came out. The man pushed himself backwards with his feet, until he hit the back wall. He moaned as he pushed himself up off the floor, staring at Lydia with wide eyes.

"Who the hell are you?" Lydia demanded, finally summoning the requisite courage.

"Keep your voice down and stay low! P-Please...my shoulder. I need a towel or something," appealed the man croakily.

Lydia, curiously relieved to have a task to complete, sprung up and made her way to the bathroom. Not wanting to leave the stranger unwatched for too long, she sprinted back. She returned to find him tentatively looking out the window. Lydia threw the towel at him and he slid back down to the ground, pressing the towel firmly to his wound.

"Who are you running from?" enquired Lydia, now feeling a rush of heat to her face.

"Stay down," insisted the man.

Lydia dropped down onto her haunches, "What is going on?" she shot back.

The stranger held up a hand that glistened red, "Can I tell you when I've finished bleeding out all over your floor?"

Lydia massaged her eyebrows, with a thumb and forefinger, "Look, you need the emergency room, not my home," she responded.

"No. No hospitals," replied the man sternly.

"At least tell me your name!" spat Lydia, her annoyance level rising.

"Dean. Dean Connors. And you are?" said Dean, extending his hand facetiously.

"L-Lydia."

"Lydia...?" Dean prompted, his eyebrows raised.

"Just Lydia."

"Fine, 'Just Lydia', I need you to do me a favor."

"Oh, in addition t-to harboring your... criminal ass?" Lydia fired back through clenched teeth, with bubbling anger that startled her.

"I'm not... I've done nothing wrong. I need you to *not* call the cops."

"Of all the... you've got to be joking!"

"I'm anything but," responded Dean, his expression darkening.

Lydia's stomach lurched and she felt the room spin again. Her anger melted away and she felt afraid for her life. She wondered if she had become some sort of magnet for bad situations. The man was in a weakened state, but he still looked dangerous. When he had stood up to full height, she guessed him to be at least six-foot tall and he had the build of a man who could both start and finish a fight. His black t-shirt was emblazoned with what looked like some sort of motorcycle brand and his jeans were torn. Was this some kind of biker drug-war thing? Frying pan refugee, you've just met the fire.

Dean examined the blood-soaked towel, "I think I've staunched the bleeding. Do you have bandages and antiseptic?" he asked, snapping Lydia back to reality.

"Uh, I'll have a look," she replied, her mind already searching for a way out.

She stopped at the dining table and discreetly picked up her phone, her back to the intruder. She shoved the phone into the waistband of her jeans.

"Hey," said Dean abruptly. Lydia stopped breathing.

"Yeah?" answered Lydia, looking back over her shoulder.

"Can you hurry?" he added.

Lydia returned to the bathroom and gently closed the door behind her. She sat on the edge of the bathtub, her right leg vibrating. She could scarcely dial the emergency services number; her fingers were sluggish and unresponsive. She lifted the phone to her ear, only to find that she had dialed '911' by mistake. What was the damned number in this country? A recorded message told her to dial '000' for the Australian emergency hotline instead. Lydia stared at the bathroom door as she fumbled with her phone; her mouth so dry, she could barely swallow let alone speak.

"Hello? Police? Lydia enquired, her voice thin and raspy.

"Please speak up if you can, Ma'am. I'm having a hard time hearing you," said the voice on the other end.

"There's a m-man. Send someone quickly, please!" whispered Lydia as loudly as she dared.

The bathroom door blew open and there stood Dean, with a look of sheer panic. He grabbed Lydia's phone and hit the call-end button.

"I asked you not to do that," he said firmly, but not angrily.

"I'm... I'm s-sorry," said Lydia shakily.

"No, I owe you an explanat-" was all Dean managed to get out, before his eyes rolled back into his head. He keeled over and landed on his back, with an almighty 'thump!'

Lydia leant over Dean's large frame; he was out cold. She grabbed his left arm and she pulled with every ounce of strength she had, but he barely budged. She inhaled and exhaled a few times before psyching herself up for another attempt. Blood rushed to her face and thumped in her ears as she tried to lift the man, but she just stumbled and tripped over his big, booted feet. 'Oh no! I'm going down!' Lydia thought, as she slammed into his body, her face inches from his.

Lydia, inexplicably, found herself studying Dean's face, which looked very different close up. He was maybe in his mid-thirties; his brown hair had natural-looking blonde streaks in it, suggesting that he spent a decent amount of time outdoors. His skin had an olive tinge; what was his heritage? There was definitely a story there. His face was unshaven, but he certainly wasn't the 'designer stubble' type. His lips: thinnish, but shapelier than they looked from a distance. Lydia had the overwhelming desire to draw Dean's face, perhaps in charcoal, to emphasize shadow and capture a potentially dark facet to his character. Wait, what was she doing?

Tingling with embarrassment, Lydia rolled off of the stranger and rose to her feet. Looking down on him now, Dean looked vulnerable and alone. Lydia wondered if he seemed that way purely because he was unconscious. People always looked kind of innocent while they slept, even the bad ones. She started racking her brain for a way to get Dean off the floor, but her brainstorming session was obliterated by a knock at the door. Was this Dean's attacker, come to finish the job? Maybe the emergency services operator was able to trace her call. Pangs of guilt hit Lydia in the gut at calling the police, but what else could she have done? She approached the door furtively and sighed heavily before opening it carefully, so that she could only just see out.

"I felt bad about leaving you here alone on your first night, pet. I brought wine!" announced Dora holding a large flagon up in the air with both hands.

"Oh-Oh! I'm... fine! No need to worry about me!" responded Lydia awkwardly.

"You okay, love? You look pale. Nothing a snout full of Dora's strawberry curative won't fix. The world's a better place when you've gotta' skin-full of wine, Lyds," chattered Dora in her sing-song voice.

"Ummm," was all Lydia could say before the pair were distracted by a vehicle pulling into the driveway behind Delilah.

Lydia grabbed at Dora's arm, trying to pull her inside, but Dora seemed unperturbed by the new arrival. Out of an unmarked sedan stepped a thick-set man, in his late forties. His greying hair had been barbered and brushed back with the precision of a swiss watch; the expression on his face was inscrutable. He slowly and deliberately meandered up the wooden stairs, toward Dora and Lydia. Lydia yanked at her sleeves, stretching them until they draped over her knuckles.

"Brian? What's 'the fuzz' doing here at this time of night? Run out of hippies to hose-down?" enquired Dora lightheartedly.

"Dora. Is this your latest tenant?" asked the policeman curtly.

"It is, yes. She's not a fugitive from the law or anything, though, Bri. You don't need to worry about her. She's a law-abiding citizen, aren't you, pet? Me, on the other hand..." quipped Dora.

"Oh, uh, Lydia. Lydia Hawkins," offered Lydia, as Brian shook her hand firmly.

"Officer Brian Barnes, but feel free to call me Brian like your landlady does. She's never been one to respect authority," said Brian with granite-like hardness.

"What's this all about?" asked Dora with a furrowed brow.

"Well, I was on my way home, when I got the call to check out your place. Something about a prowler?" said Brian looking directly at Lydia.

"A prowler!" repeated Dora with eyes like dinner plates.

"I should come on through and have a look around the place, Ms. Hawkins," said Brian with an air of command.

"Oh Lydia, you poor thing. You must be out of your mind with panic!" gushed Dora.

Lydia couldn't look Brian in the eyes. She wasn't sure what to do now that he was here at her doorstep. She looked at Dora, who now appeared puzzled by Lydia's demeanor.

"Oh, it's fine. I'm so sorry. It must have been a... trick of the light," said Lydia apologetically.

"Are you certain, pet?" asked Dora.

"Yeah, I think it's best if I take a look around," affirmed Brian.

"No!" replied Lydia, suddenly sensing that her protest was a little too forceful, "I mean, new house, new country. I'm just jumpy is all. I'm sorry to have wasted your time, Officer Barnes, uh, Brian."

"Oh well, do you want a splash of my homemade strawberry concoction, Bri? Seeing as how you've come all this way," suggested Dora playfully.

"No thanks Dora. I've heard about your concoctions and apparently they're like you: forceful and volatile!" Brian spat sarcastically.

"Well, if you want to be a killjoy, how about a cup of herbal tea?" countered Dora.

"But, I've got to show you that *thing*, remember Dora?" quickly interjected Lydia.

"The what? Oh, the thing!" replied Dora, quickly picking up Lydia's thread.

"Well, if everything's okay," said Brian, scowling, his small, dark eyes scanning the front yard.

"Certainly is," added Lydia.

"Well, I'll leave you my number. Anything out of the ordinary, you call me, alright?" said Brian, with an expression that suggested he wasn't entirely convinced. He whipped out a small, spiral notepad and jotted down his cell number. Ripping out the page, he handed it to Lydia. He started down the stairs, then stopped and spun around.

"Anything. Tricks of the light included. We've been getting some bad types in the area lately," asserted Brian, before heading to his car.

Dora waited for Brian to pull out of the driveway, before turning to Lydia, "Cute, right?" she said conspiratorially.

"I guess, if you're into vaguely crabby, older men," replied Lydia.

"Oh, I like 'em old, young, tall, short. Just not too talkative. I can't stand a chatterbox. They drive me up the wall, with all that gum flapping. There's nothing worse than verbal diarrhea, love."

"Well, you're going to love what I've got to show you then," said Lydia with a half-smile.

"Oh, so there really is a 'thing', is there?"

"More like a *him*," replied Lydia.

"Okay, outta' my way," commanded Dora comically, pushing her way in.

Dora stomped down the hallway and lobbed her belongings onto the dining table.

"I've just gotta' hit the little girl's room, before you reveal your naughty little secrets to mistress Dora," she stated theatrically, as she rounded the corner into the alcove, just outside the bathroom. She stopped dead in her tracks when she laid eyes on Dean's outstretched body. She was still standing there, staring, when Lydia loomed up behind her.

"He's the *thing*," Lydia stated flatly.

"Who is this man? Is he your intruder? Lyds? Oh, my giddy aunt! You shot him!" blurted Dora.

"How on earth would I have gotten a gun into the country?" quizzed Lydia, taken back by the inference.

"He's not dead, is he? Wait, you're not denying that you *have* fired a gun at some point?"

"I've fired the odd warning shot or two, just to protect the chickens... when I was much younger," replied Lydia sheepishly.

"You're full of surprises, petal. Okay, the shock's worn off... slightly. What should we do with 'the wild one' here?"

"Let's get him up onto the couch, I guess," suggested Lydia.

"What do you think he weighs? A hundred kilos? That's... more than two hundred pounds! Alright, I'm glad I ate my porridge this morning. Let's haul this beast!" declared Dora.

Lydia gawkily took hold of Dean's legs and Dora grabbed his wrists tightly.

"Ready? Up!" shouted Dora as they lifted Dean off the ground.

The pair unceremoniously dragged, twisted and pulled Dean's limp body, until they had him near the sofa. With one final, determined exertion, they hoisted him up onto the softness of the couch. Breathing heavily, Lydia and Dora admired their efforts.

"You know, he's not bad looking," said Dora mischievously.

Lydia glanced at Dean and then back at Dora, "Who? Him?"

"Of course, him, pet. How many hunks are you hiding in here?"

"Oh, I wouldn't say-"

"You don't have to, love. Mystic Dora sees all."

"I have to say, you're taking this all rather well. A strange man with a bullet-wound on your property? Anyone else would be, I don't know, more upset," said Lydia.

"Like I said, Mystic Dora sees all, particularly that injury. There's a first aid kit under the sink."

Lydia returned with the medical supplies to find Dora examining Dean's shoulder. "There's an exit hole luckily. No need to fish out the slug," said Dora nonchalantly.

"Now who's full of surprises?" Lydia asked.

"Volunteering in Africa, pet. I've seen the odd gun-shot wound. We'll have to, ahh, get his shirt off," stated Dora with a grin.

Lydia pursed her lips, "'Course we do," she stated.

Lydia pulled Dean forward and Dora lifted his bloodied shirt over his head. There were scars on his torso; it looked like he'd been stabbed and cut more than once. There were some tattoos as well; Lydia couldn't make them out and she didn't want to stare, but she couldn't help but admire what looked like a phoenix in the middle of his chest. Lydia found herself pondering how long something like that would take to get inscribed on somebody's flesh. This man was no stranger to pain, that much was certain.

Out of the first aid kit, Dora pulled some antiseptic and cleaned up the wound, "The bleeding's stopped," said Dora as she sewed up the entry hole. She then took a dressing and applied it expertly, repeating the process for the exit wound.

"He'll be alright, I think," said Dora.

"Good. That's good," replied Lydia.

Dora placed a jangly hand on her hip, "Still need to get him to a doctor. When he's well en-"

Lydia cut in, "No doctors, he said. He insisted. I don't think he's the kind of guy you make angry."

"So, you've been getting acquainted, then?"

"Not by choice," replied Lydia.

Dora touched Lydia's hand, "Oh pet, he gave you a right old scare, did he?"

"He was uninvited, that's all."

"Well, there's one thing I can tell you: his aura is pure as the driven snow, 'far as I can see. He might be into some bad business, but he's a pussycat deep down, this one," cooed Dora as she stroked Dean's unmoving arm.

"I've been fooled before," Lydia responded coldly.

"Well, if you don't want him, he's mine then," said Dora with a wink.

"You're welcome to him. I'm going to wash his shirt. The sooner he's out of here, the better," Lydia said before leaving the room.

"What are you running from?" whispered Dora into Dean's ear.

MASON'S MOUTH WAS BONE-dry and his leathery tongue stuck to the roof of it. When he slowly opened his eyes, he was accosted by searing pain in his skull. He tried to lift his head but his neck was unresponsive. Thoughts came slowly, just images at first, pictures of the previous night. He remembered dinner: eye fillet, cooked rare, just the way he liked it. He could almost smell the garlic in the creamy aligot island, surrounded by an ocean of glossy, beef jus. There was red wine also, but not so much that he should feel as toxic as he did. What the hell happened?

After some experimentation, he found that he could move by rolling his body slowly. Gritting his teeth, Mason forced his body to the left as hard as he could. He rolled twice, before the bed seemed to fall way and the next thing he knew, he was on the ground, wedged between the bed and a chest of hardwood drawers. His whole body ached, not in a good way, like the day or two after adding more weight to his bench-press sessions. Mason ached like someone who had been stumbling around the desert for a week, not that he had even seen a desert before. He was so thirsty; he fantasized about a cold mountain stream, coursing its way down the street, through the bedroom window and into his open mouth. Then a wave of nausea came over him, but he beat it back with sheer force of will; he was not about to vomit on his own bedroom floor. Darkness.

Mason awoke to pins and needles in his left arm; he must have dropped off, but for how long? It wasn't as bright as when he first woke up; some hours must have gone by, he guessed. With much effort and by dragging himself up with the aid of his dresser drawers, Mason finally pulled himself to his feet. He hobbled to the bathroom, urinated and washed his hands. He splashed cool water on his face, took a long drink and studied his reflection in the mirror. His blue eyes were puffy and bloodshot; his skin looked sallow and sickly. His black hair was pasted onto his forehead and his thick beard dripped water onto the sink. He wasn't at his best, that was for sure. Was this food poisoning? The beef was only cooked briefly, but then he would have picked up on it if it was rotten. He was always very astute when it came to things like that. He knew when that douche of a waiter, at the French place in town, had lied about the meat being locally sourced. He could taste those food miles; no one could put one over on Mason and his perfectly honed palette.

Memories of the night's events now came rushing back at Mason, like water from a faucet. Sitting at the table, looking across at her, her cagey glances, back at him. She was wearing the dress he'd bought her, for the anniversary of when she'd finally moved in with him. She looked pretty decent in red, he'd always told her. She said that she agreed, but he could tell she was just placating him. He'd put on some Mozart: The Marriage of Figaro. She always grimaced a little when she heard it, but the girl never did have any taste. There were flowers in a vase on the side-table; they were irises. The flowers were her choice, he didn't care. He knew that her mom liked irises. The few times they'd met, she'd waffled on and on about them. She kept at him, about how good the soil in Boulder was for Bearded Irises, joking about how that should be her daughter's pet name for Mason. The Bearded Iris? Come on, lady. He preferred what they had called him in high school: 'The Wall'. It was not only a play on his surname: Wahl, but recognition of his toughness and he liked that.

Where was she? What day was it? Tuesday? He stroked his beard repeatedly. No, it was Wednesday; he knew that because she wasn't there. She was at home the four days prior, including the weekend, so it had to be Wednesday. She worked the last three days of the week, at that art supply store; it was the 'closest she would ever get to the art world', she would always say. She'd begged and begged him to let her work there. He had held out as long as he could, but she wore him down. The idea of her spending all that time away from him, made Mason's blood run cold. Why would she want to get away? Who would she be working with? Would she be flirting with other men? But Mason had soon come to realize that she was too scared to even look at other guys. The fact that she had her own job, meant that Mason had the opportunity for a little privacy, seeing as how his consultation business saw him working from home. She needed him, needed his strength and his money and his love. She was so helpless, like a little lamb.

Mason belched and tasted wine. The wine. It was a cabernet sauvignon, from the Napa Valley; he'd been saving it, but there was a little leakage through the cork and Mason had worried that it may become oxidized. He'd carefully decanted it and left it to breathe for an hour before dinner. She never cared about wine, not like he did. She couldn't tell the difference between a cab sav and a merlot. When he'd met her, he thought her ignorance was cute. He'd tease her about being a farmgirl and her lack of sophistication and she'd laugh, but he could see she was embarrassed. Her face would go red and he'd joke that she'd just turned the color of pinot noir, not that she would even know what that was.

She knew what last night's bottle was though; she'd asked him: 'Do you want another g-glass of cabernet?' in her nervous little voice. The wine! She never referred to wine by its variety. She was so accommodating last night, wasn't she; topping up his glass at every turn. He'd enjoyed it at the time, but now he saw her deceit so clearly. She'd drugged the damn wine! She'd left him for dead and now she was who-knows-where, probably shacked up with some lover! "Lydiaaaaaaaaa!" yelled Mason at the top of his voice. He punched the glass of the bathroom cabinet, shattering it.

DEAN ROSE EARLY IN the morning; his shuffling woke Lydia as she was a light sleeper. Dora was still snoring in the spare room; Lydia had insisted she stay over after they'd managed to finish the flagon of - very strong - wine. Lydia was still haunted by remnants of what tasted like strawberry jam and nail polish remover, as she brushed her teeth. She ruminated on the best way of approaching Dean, as she did her best to look presentable. Lydia wasn't keen on the idea of showering with a strange man in the house; it didn't feel right somehow, being naked near him.

"Do you... have my shirt?" Dean enquired, as he and Lydia met in the hallway. He looked endearingly self -conscious, Lydia thought.

"Yes, I washed it last night. It should be dry by now. Good thing about the tropics." Lydia quickly jostled past Dean and went out into the backyard.

The shirt was being gently teased on the clothesline, by a sultry morning breeze. Lydia pulled the garment down and poked her finger through the bullet hole. The only good thing about the whole episode with Dean, was that it had taken her mind off of Mason for a short while. Mason. Had she left any loose ends? Lydia took inventory of everything she had chosen to leave behind. There was nothing that pointed to her coming to Australia. She had purchased her plane ticket with cash and she hadn't spoken about her plans with anyone, save for Dora and Kitty. She hadn't told her sister too much; she was trustworthy, but it was for her own safety. Kitty had wanted to come with her. Lydia would have let her if it wasn't for Mom; Lydia hated leaving her in that place. Her mind was going, dementia they said it was and the thought of it hurt Lydia's heart. Dad was a hard man, right up until the day he died, but Mom was always gentle and sort of delicate; she didn't deserve a decline like the one she'd been struck with. Lydia hoped that Kitty had followed her instructions. No, she had been careful; he would never find her.

Lydia began to fold the t-shirt as she walked back to the house; was she being too familiar? She tried throwing it over her shoulder casually. Was that what one of Dean's mates would do? Not too many mates would launder his shirts, she guessed. Lydia entered the back door to find Dora doting on Dean; geez, that lady worked fast. Lydia felt a peculiar discomfort in her chest; like someone had jammed a knitting needle in it. Was she, dare she say it: jealous?

"Well, top of the morning, petal! Mr. Connors and I are just getting acquainted. I hear that you've already met Lydia Hawkins, my dear boy," Dora hollered.

"Yes. We've certainly met," said Dean, smiling at Lydia. Lydia looked at the ceiling, then at Dora.

"How did you pull up after last night?" prodded Dora enthusiastically.

"A little dusty, but all in one piece. You sound like you feel better than me, though. What was in that stuff?"

"Love, petal. I make the stuff with oodles of love. That and copious quantities of alcohol," replied Dora gleefully.

Dora peered into Lydia's eyes, pausing momentarily, "I'm going to take off, love. People to do, things to see and all that. Now you really must come and see my stall at the night markets, Dean. I'll do you a discount on a full-body rub, with a chakra realignment thrown in."

Lydia looked back at Dora pleadingly, "You don't want to stay a while and chat?"

"Come and see me out," replied Dora, already making for the front door.

Lydia tugged at Dora's arm, a look of alarm on her face, "What do I do with... him?" she whispered urgently.

Dora clutched Lydia's hands, "Let the Goddess guide you, my love," she said.

"The who?" asked Lydia.

"Don't let him wander around your kitchen half naked though, pet. You'll get a reputation," joked Dora, pointing at the black t-shirt still draped over Lydia's shoulder.

Lydia watched her friend drive away, trying to delay the inevitable interaction with her 'guest'. She dragged her feet back to the kitchen and found Dean closing the shutters on each window.

"Leave that one open," instructed Lydia, throwing Dean his shirt.

Dean twisted around and caught the projectile. "Why?"

"I don't want to miss seeing the Cook-a-burry," she said shyly.

Dean cocked an eyebrow, "The Cook-a-what? Oh, you mean kookaburra," he said, with a chuckle, as he put on his shirt.

Lydia paused for a moment, listening for cruelty in his voice, but found none.

"Okay," Lydia responded, looking at the floor, "N-Now I know."

"I'm sorry about all of this. Trust me, it's not something I usually do: forcing myself into someone's house. I just want to say thank you, especially for not calling the cops," Dean said.

"Actually," began Lydia.

Dean interrupted, "Look, I'm not a bad person. I was a bit of a dumb kid that just sorta' ended up rolling with some hard... guys," he said, editing his language for Lydia's sake.

"You don't have to explain," Lydia offered.

"No, no. I came bursting into *your* life. You deserve the truth." Dean began pacing. "I was part of a biker gang – The Wild Colonial Boys – you heard of them?"

"No. I've only been in Australia for a day," Lydia replied. "I haven't had a chance to get to know all the gangs in town, yet."

"Oh. Okay. Well they're renowned around here for being... well, pretty badass. The truth of it is: they're just criminals. There's no two ways about it. I started out feeling tough when I was with them, that and I felt like I belonged somewhere, like I mattered. I guess it was like a tribe. We looked out for one another. But at the end of the day, we were sorta' thugs too and I couldn't take it anymore, so I left and that's when the proverbial hit the fan."

"That's tough. I mean, really tough, to walk away like that," Lydia said sincerely.

"Well now is when things get really tough. But that's not your problem. I've taken up enough of your time, Lydia. Can I give you some money?" Dean pulled out his wallet, secured to his belt with a thick, silver chain.

"You certainly cannot," replied Lydia, mildly offended.

"I'm sorry, I've just had you patching me up, washing my clothes. I didn't mean to put your nose out of joint," Dean pleaded.

"No, I mean, a person can simply do something good for someone else without needing to be rewarded. Maybe I'm naïve."

"Better naïve than bitter, huh?" countered Dean.

"I guess. Want something to eat?"

"I'd be lying if I said I wasn't hungry as a bear with a tapeworm," Dean answered with an easy smile.

Chapter Three

The Escapists

Dean offered to cook but Lydia insisted he rest, what with being shot up and all. Dora had left bacon, eggs and a selection of mushrooms in the fridge, "I love you too, 'pet'" Lydia whispered as the, very substantial looking, Australian bacon hit the cast iron pan and sizzled enticingly. She looked over at Dean every so often as she prepared breakfast; he smiled at her every time, which Lydia found a little weird. Slowly, she noticed how pleasant a smile the man actually had; he looked genuinely happy to be in her company. Lydia put it down to loss of blood.

As Lydia set things out on the dining table, the sleeve of her dressing gown rode up. She quickly sat and pulled the sleeves down to her wrists, but not before Dean noticed the bruising. He was quiet suddenly and his smile faded. He held her gaze for a moment, as though he was trying to read her thoughts. The contents of his mind were on his face. He appeared to understand what he had just seen and it was clear that he was angered by it.

"How long did that go on for?" he asked sullenly.

"Did what go on for? It's nothing, just moving and everything," mumbled Lydia.

"You know what I mean. Those bruises aren't from moving house."

Lydia smoothed her sleeves out, "Just... let's eat, okay. Forget it," she pleaded. Dean picked at his plate whilst still staring at Lydia.

"I can't forget it," Dean finally replied.

"I'm not going to talk to *you* about that," snapped Lydia.

Dean clenched a fist, "Bastard needs a good punch in the chops," he said hotly.

Lydia dropped her utensils onto her plate, "How do you know that it was a 'bastard'. Maybe I do extreme sports," she said in riposte.

"Experience. Seen it before. It's not just the bruises that tell the story, it's in the eyes of the person on the receiving end. If ever I saw any of the guys in the gang doing that kind of thing, well, I put a stop to it," Dean said grimly. "Hitting women is a low act."

Lydia looked away and then back at Dean, "L-look, I'm not a little lamb that needs protecting, ok?" she retorted. Little lamb? Mason had called her that; his 'scared little lamb'. It made her sick now that she was regurgitating his words.

"I'm just telling it like it is," replied Dean. "And you're not the extreme sports type."

Lydia slammed a palm on the table, "You're so frustrating! Who made you the expert on how things are? Why would I want to talk about this?" she spat.

Dean held both hands up in a gesture of surrender, "Okay, I can see that you're upset. I'd better push off, I think."

"Maybe that'd be best," said Lydia, folding her arms and looking toward the hallway.

"Thanks for everything anyway. I appreciate what you did for me. Anyone else would have probably turfed me out onto the footpath, or had me picked up by the jacks."

Lydia glared angrily at her plate. She turned in time to see Dean, disappearing down the hallway, like a wounded animal. He was hunched over and looked dejected. Part of her wanted to call him back, but she was still unhappy about him sticking his nose in her business. She didn't want pity or protection; she wanted to feel normal again. How could she be a better version of herself, if people kept handling her like she might break at any moment?

THE REST OF THE DAY was spent making slight adjustments to furniture settings, wandering the house and picking at what was left in the fridge. Lydia leafed through a book entitled: 'Finding Your Inner Witch' and she couldn't help but laugh; maybe she could turn the next man who intruded on her life, into a toad. Dora would have been quick to correct Lydia, if she was around. Dora was quick to expound on the virtues of Paganism and Wicca. Lydia felt a flash of mild envy; if only she knew herself and what she wanted, like Dora did. It would take time if it were to happen at all; time away from the negative gravitational pull of Mason and his constant criticism. But first, Lydia really desired some time all to herself. A surge of panic hit her all of a sudden; what if people from Dean's gang had seen where he was hiding the night before? An unwanted visit from violent thugs; the mere thought horrified Lydia. Then again, what if they'd followed Dean home, or to wherever he had ended up? Lydia locked the front and back doors, employing every chain and latch. She found Officer Barnes' number and secured it to the fridge door with a magnet.

Late in the afternoon, her friend: the 'kookaburra', showed up. Lydia had looked up foods that the funny little bird might eat, on her phone. She saved some meat for him and cut it into thin strips that were meant to look like little snakes. She threw a slice to the kookaburra and surprisingly, he caught it in his beak from his branch. He smacked the meat against the tree, 'killing' it, before gobbling it down. His head seemed too big for his body and Lydia giggled at him, feeling bad afterward. She then pulled out her sketch pad and some charcoal and stood there sketching 'little big-head', until she found herself turning over to a fresh page.

Lydia sketched and rubbed, shaded and rendered furiously, for at least twenty minutes before she grasped what she was actually doing. Dean's face, with that easy smile, presented itself to her on the page. It wasn't a rough approximation of his face, it was a faithful rendering of the man himself. Lydia gawked at the drawing for some time, before snapping the sketch pad shut. There was a feeling in the pit of her stomach, but it wasn't fear or dread; she knew those feelings intimately. This was something else, something she hadn't felt in a long time. Was this homesickness? No, it wasn't longing for what had been; if Lydia was brutally honest, this was anticipation for things to come.

THE EVENING WENT UNINTERRUPTED and Lydia turned in early. The night's sleep was another story altogether; dreams came hard and fast. In her dreams, she was alone in the darkness at the outset. She would feel around for something, anything, to tell her how to escape the void. But then she would feel a presence, something else in the vacuum, approaching her ominously. A sliver of light would slice through the blackness and standing there, looming over her, was Mason. He was twelve feet tall and wild like some giant from a fairytale. His eyes glowed red and his lips parted to reveal a gaping maw full of cruel, jagged teeth. Then he was lumbering around Lydia's new house, throwing furniture about, madly searching for her. She tried to run, but her legs were too heavy. She wanted to scream, but no voice came. Dora appeared, materializing like smoke turned solid, rushing up from gaps in the floorboards; her hands outstretched like a sorceress conjuring some protective spell. The giant Mason picked her up with one hand; he was even bigger now, as though his rage was making him swell. He thrust Dora's tiny body into his slavering mouth and ate her. Dean was there too, but he was passed out on the floor; a metal spike rising up from the ground like a stalagmite, plunging its way through the back of his shoulder.

Lydia awoke the next morning, drenched with sweat and exhausted. This was the way the next few days transpired: meandering through the sunlight hours to be persecuted by demons in the darkness. On a morning when Lydia felt the nagging pain of loneliness beginning to make its presence known, she stepped out of the shower to a persistent and very familiar sound. She threw on some clothes and strolled out into the backyard to find Dean, chopping firewood as though it were the most normal thing in the world.

"What are you doing?" she called out.

Dean stopped chopping and threw the axe up onto his shoulder, "Morning, Lydia. Just returning a favor. Getting you prepped for winter," he stated.

"Y-you can't just come over and start doing stuff in my backyard, whenever you want, you know!"

"Oh, sorry. It's just how we sorta' do things around here. I can come back later if you're busy," Dean said casually.

"Y-You're going to tear your stitches!" Lydia suggested.

"Feels fine. Your friend did a bang-up job. Tell her I said so," Dean volleyed back.

Some part of Lydia felt happy for the company and Dean continued chopping anyway. She watched him heaving the large axe, glistening with perspiration, looking perfectly at home. Lydia couldn't help but admire his self-confidence, in fact, she was downright jealous of it. Dean winced a little with every other stroke of the axe, but Lydia could tell that he was playing down the pain. Was he trying to impress her?

"Does this place even have a winter?" she yelled, trying to sound more convivial.

"Well, summer's almost over. In a few short months, it'll start getting cooler," answered Dean, not missing a beat.

"What minimum temperatures should I be prepared for?"

"Wow, you're looking at around eight degrees at night to... about twenty-one in the day."

"That's Celsius, right? Do you know what that would be in Fahrenheit?"

Dean thought for a moment, "That's around... forty-six to about sixty-four?"

Lydia thought back to winters in Colorado and smiled, "I think I'll manage, but thanks for the effort."

"No wuckers," Dean replied in his broad Australian accent.

"Wuckers?" Lydia questioned.

"It's short for: no 'wucken furries'. Meaning: no fu-" Dean stopped himself.

Lydia placed her hands on her hips, "Meaning what, exactly," she quizzed, with mock disapproval.

"Just means: no worries," said Dean, with the beginnings of a grin.

Lydia laughed and she could see a look of satisfaction on Dean's face, like he was proud of himself for cheering her up.

"You come on in, when you're hungry," offered Lydia.

"Well, I was wondering. Wondering if you might want to come over to mine for dinner tonight?"

"I, ummm," Lydia muttered.

"I'm not a terrible cook and I promise, no funny stuff," said Dean straightforwardly.

"Oh, sorry, but I'm hanging out with Dora tonight," lied Lydia.

"Okay. That's cool. Open invitation. I'll probably chuck a line in tonight anyway. Catch a Kingfish or two."

"Never took you for a fisherman," Lydia said,

"I'm not. I don't know why I said that," laughed Dean.

"I'll see you later, Dean. Thanks for the wood."

"I'll leave my number in your letter box. Call me if you change your mind about dinner."

"I'll put it on the fridge... add it to the collection," Lydia returned.

"Bye, Lydia," Dean said as he dropped the axe, wedging it back into the chopping block where he found it.

Lydia cursed herself, "I'll add it to the collection?" she repeated. She hoped Dean didn't take that to mean she was amassing a collection of phone numbers from other men. Why was she worried about that? This was getting silly. She paced up and down, painstakingly scrutinizing every word of her exchange with Dean. Had she said the wrong things? She'd yelled at the guy, but he was taking liberties, right? Maybe they did do things differently out here. She would have to get used to her surroundings sooner or later, but in her own time. Outside, an engine started and a vehicle pulled out of the driveway.

Lydia ran to the front door, undid the latches and made for the front steps. She'd half hoped that she might stop Dean from driving away but he was gone. Lydia pulled back the metal lid of the mailbox and found the phone number that Dean had left for her; it was written on a napkin, probably from some fast food joint. Lydia took her prize back inside and attached it to the refrigerator door, as promised. Dean had drawn a smiley face, with its tongue poking out, under the digits of his cell. Lydia imagined what Dean's tongue might feel like, before snapping herself out of it with a jolt. She opened the fridge door and took out some chilled water. Cooling down, that's what she needed.

AFTER BUSYING HERSELF with day to day tasks, Lydia sat, absent-mindedly caressing the screen of her phone. She found herself thinking wistfully about home and picturing the faces of her mom and sister. A voice from home would really put things into perspective.

"Katherine?"

"Hey Listeria!" Kitty bubbled.

Lydia shook her head, "You still calling me that, huh?"

"I'll stop when it stops being funny, also, when did you start calling me Katherine? What's happening? Is your place nice? Have you met anyone?"

"One thing at a time, lady. You're fine, right? You're still at Donna's? You haven't seen, what's his name," Lydia said seriously.

"No, no, everything's cool. Answer my questions!" Kitty said with a laugh in her voice.

"The place is beautiful. It's warm here, very warm. If you were here, you'd be thrown in jail for indecent exposure. I saw the ocean for the first time, which was, really something. I miss you and Mom, though. I miss you a lot," said Lydia, suppressing a sob.

"Hey, we're still here. We'll see each other again, Listy. Just like old times," said Kitty consolingly.

"Thanks Kitty, I needed to hear that."

"Sure. Now, let's see, what did you leave out? Oh! Men!"

"You are the worst!" Lydia replied.

"Yeah, yeah. Tell me!"

"There might be a guy. I don't know. It's too weird."

"Lydia. You need to start thinking about what *you* want. God, you've been sorta' on hold for a lotta' years. If you don't start living now, then when will you?"

"I'm supposed to be looking out for *you*. I'm the big sister. I feel like a failure," Lydia said sadly.

"Remember when our stupid cousin used to visit, when we were eight or nine?"

Lydia rubbed her forehead, "Gilbert?"

"Yeah, that idiot. The one who used to eat his boogers and say, 'Now that hit the spot!' afterward."

"How could I forget?"

"Well do you remember what he used to do to me, like, all the time?"

"I remember him pulling his... thing... out. He used to wave it at you. Weird little pervert."

"Well, yeah. Remember there was one day when I'd had enough and I cried and that's when you got mad."

"Maybe."

"Well you did and then the next time he treated me to an exhibition, you pulled a switch from a spruce tree, just like Dad used to and whacked his little doo-dad with it. When he cried, you told him that you'd trained our cat – Ulysses – to eat wieners. You convinced him, that if he told anyone about his punishment, you'd sic Ulysses on him. You'd even stand outside the bathroom when he was peeing and make cat noises. Little jerk didn't squeeze another drop til' the ride home."

"Oh my God. I'd completely forgotten about that," said Lydia laughing.

"Thing is, you've always looked after me, Lydia. You're so much stronger than you give yourself credit for. All the same, let me look out for you, for once."

"I'll think about it," replied Lydia quietly.

"Don't think. Do. That's what Mom would tell you, if she... you know."

"Stop it Kitty, you're gonna' make me cry again."

"You've done enough crying. Anyway, that's enough soppy stuff. Rope yourself a new dude!"

"Oh, don't change," said Lydia.

A DAY WENT BY BEFORE Lydia had the courage to even look at Dean's number. Even then, she would dial part of it, put the phone down and walk away. It was midday before she drummed up enough verve to call the man. When he answered, she nearly hung up like a schoolgirl calling her crush. But when she heard his voice, something in her took over. Lydia wasn't even sure of what she was saying, but the conversation ended with, "I'll see you at five."

That evening, Lydia spread out some clothing options on the bed; there wasn't much to choose from. Over the years, her outfits had become more about coverage and practicality than anything else. Dean had already seen what she was trying to hide from the world, but she still had no desire to spark up another debate about her past life. She settled on a dark, long-sleeved dress and black tights; Lydia knew she'd be uncomfortable in the heat, but protected from prying eyes nonetheless. She tried on some shoes; luckily Dora had left some in the bedroom closet. Dora had more shoes than she could wear in a lifetime, she'd always said. Dora and Lydia were the same exact shoe size somehow; good thing she had big feet for a little lady. Lydia tried some black wedges that would give her some height. Maybe she shouldn't go at all; what did she think was going to happen?

Before she had too much time for internal struggle, Dean pulled up outside in a big pickup. She liked that he had insisted on coming to get her; it was old-fashioned and it would save her the worry of wandering around town, advertising her presence. Mason was never one for picking her up or even considering how she would get to their joint destination, when they were dating. Dating. This was a date, wasn't it? The word bounced around Lydia's head for a moment, until Dean knocked on the front door. Lydia opened up to a fresh-looking version of the man she'd met twice before. He was wearing a light, collared shirt and a variation on the jeans he seemed to like. His hair was all brushed back and wet-looking and he smelled like sandalwood and leather.

"You look nice," was the first thing he said.

"You too, for a biker," Lydia replied, instantly regretting her words.

"Ex-biker," Dean corrected.

"So, we heading off?" said Lydia, trying to break any possible tension.

"Ready when you are, Lydia," replied Dean, bowing and motioning her out the door ceremoniously.

Dean opened the passenger-side door for Lydia. The truck smelled like him, but with the addition of something else: lumber or sawdust perhaps. Lydia felt pressured to make small talk, but the roar of the engine took care of that, thankfully. On the drive to Dean's place, Lydia was free to take in her surroundings. Dean would occasionally point to the odd place of interest and Lydia would smile approvingly. There was something effortless in Dean's manner and it put Lydia at ease. Try as she might, Lydia couldn't imagine this version of the man, getting up to no good with a gang.

"Just making a stop first," Dean announced suddenly as he pulled the truck into a laneway.

"Ooookay," responded Lydia, a little unsure of how to react.

Dean threw open his door and rounded the vehicle to open Lydia's, "Won't take long. Promise," said Dean.

Lydia had to jump out of the very tall truck to the ground below. Dean rooted through his keys until he found the one he wanted, plunging it into a huge padlock that secured a metal door with a thick chain. He pulled back the door to reveal a large space, a workshop, that smelled of wood-shavings and the sharp sting of lacquer. Dean gestured and Lydia entered to find a world of impeccably crafted wooden pieces that were less furniture than they were works of art.

"Doing some shopping?" Lydia asked.

"You like my stuff?" Dean countered.

"You made these?" Lydia gasped.

"Yeah, I dabble," Dean laughed.

"These are incredible," Lydia said in awe.

"Thanks. They're not bad."

"They're better than not bad. They're pretty good," ribbed Lydia.

"I've never shown another living soul my stuff, you know."

"I'm honored Mr. Connors," replied Lydia.

"Please. You can call me: Master Craftsman Connors," jibed Dean.

Lydia was drawn to a meticulously crafted chair in the corner of the room; she padded over to it gently as though she was afraid of spooking it. The high back featured carvings of satyrs and other mythic creatures and in the center: a maiden. The woman was beautiful; naked but classical and tasteful.

"Ah, you've got good taste. That one's my passion project," Dean said, perambulating up to the chair and stroking it with an air of pride.

"It... magnificent," said Lydia wistfully.

"Nice of you to say, but now that you've seen my inner sanctum, you'll be doing the dishes after dinner." Lydia shot Dean a hard stare and followed it up with a firm smack on the arm.

"Okay, Okay. No dishes," responded Dean, rubbing his arm for dramatic effect, "You sure *you're* not in a gang?"

DEAN GENTLY TOUCHED Lydia's shoulder, wakening her from an impromptu nap.

"How long was I out?" she asked groggily.

"Almost the whole journey. Must have been the aromas of the workshop. Can't have been my sparkling personality," quipped Dean.

Lydia looked side to side, "We're here?" she questioned.

"Yep. Castle Connors. Forgive the chaos will you."

"Chaos? You're on the water?" Lydia said, exiting the truck and stumbling towards a sublime ocean view.

"Yeah, it's a bit much isn't it. Ill-gotten gains and all that. I'm selling up soon; moving in above the workshop."

Lydia looked back at Dean, "Oh. That's a shame."

"Is it, now," replied Dean with a chuckle.

On entering the house, Lydia guessed that it had only ever been inhabited by Dean. There were easy chairs of dark, brown leather and stacks of books on the floor. An eclectic mix of handmade furniture adorned each room that Dean presented to her. There were exquisitely framed paintings of the seaside everywhere, filling almost every available space and even propped up against the walls; Lydia wondered for a moment whether Dean had painted them. She was wary of asking too many questions, or seeming too interested. Scattered sketches of what looked like furniture concept designs, were stacked and scattered on most flat surfaces. Lydia had always theorized that much is learned about a person by examining their living space; Dean's house was the gallery of a dreamer.

"Can I get you a drink, Lydia?"

"I wouldn't say no to a white wine, if you have some," Lydia replied, still trying to absorb her surroundings.

"I think I might have something," said Dean, disappearing into the kitchen.

"You're a real artiste," called Lydia, loudly enough to be heard in the next room.

"I've been called worse," Dean said, returning with a glass of something cold.

"No, really. I don't want you to get a big head, but you've got a lot of talent."

"And you haven't even tasted my duck yet," Dean replied.

"Duck?" repeated Lydia, her eyes widening.

"He's just gone back into the oven. Shouldn't be long, he's already spent some time roasting today. He's a twice-cooked bird, he's just got to crisp up. Now we've got time for a stroll. Bring your drink."

THE SALTY AIR TEASED Lydia's hair, as the pair walked along the beach, that was right outside Dean's home. The sun was disappearing and the sky was painted in shades of orange and crimson. The sound of waves crashing on the shore drove Lydia to distraction and before long, she had kicked off her shoes and broken out into a run towards the water. Dean followed, jogging to keep up, but all Lydia could focus on was the ocean, spread before her like an ever-moving, never-ending lake. As her feet met the shock of cold seawater, Lydia giggled like a child, kicking her feet in all directions. Water was quickly absorbed by the material of her tights and it travelled up her legs, but she didn't care. She turned to look at Dean who was smiling at her admiringly it seemed; she beamed back at him. A small wave arched its back behind Lydia and smashed against her legs, wetting the back of her dress. Lydia was so giddy, in the embrace of her new experience, that she hadn't even noticed the contents of her glass spilling, as she skipped about.

Dean entered the water slowly, approaching Lydia carefully as though at any moment he might accidentally snap her out of her blissful state, "Not much water where you're from, I take it?"

"Boulder? Nothing like this."

"Colorado's a beautiful place I hear."

"It is," replied Lydia, her face tensing slightly, "This is better!" Her invigorated demeanor returned as she flicked salty water at Dean.

"It's like that is it?" challenged Dean whimsically, lunging forward to chase Lydia.

Lydia squealed and ran away as fast as she could, through the incoming waves. She ran in a zig-zag to avoid capture, but Dean was too fast. Before she knew it, they had collided like wave on shore. She was locked in a swift, potent embrace and time slowed, as they came face to face. Lydia could feel Dean's breath and the hardness of his body against hers. The roughness of his stubbled chin, made Lydia's skin tingle. Dean's lips found hers; Lydia's eyes closed instinctively and the world disappeared.

Chapter Four

Engulfed

A feeling rose up in Lydia, like poison from a snake-bite; it was so powerful that she broke away from Dean, pushing hard on his chest. Dean looked puzzled; his eyes then narrowed and he looked out to sea.

"Too much, too soon, huh?" he seemed to ask into the air.

Lydia looked down at the water, "No funny business. It's what you promised, back at my house."

Dean lifted Lydia's head with a forefinger under her chin, "Nothing funny about it, Lydia."

"It's just... the duck," Lydia offered, with very little confidence.

Lydia began the walk back to the house and Dean followed after her. The pair walked in silence, the sound of the waves on the shore slowly fading behind them. As soon as they re-entered the house, Dean made a beeline for the oven. He busied himself in the kitchen, clanging plates and things methodically, for longer than he needed to. Lydia sat at the mahogany dining table, her chair turned toward the glass ocean-side sliding door, that opened straight out onto the beach. She jumped when Dean plopped a large oven-dish, onto a cane mat, on the table with one hand, plates and cutlery with the other.

"My duck is legendary. Prepare to enter the temple of taste," stated Dean theatrically.

He deftly carved pieces off of the whole roast duck, serving Lydia first. When both plates had been filled with meat and a selection of glistening, roasted vegetables, he motioned for Lydia to eat. She took a bite and then another. Lydia wanted to compliment Dean on his cooking, especially after her reaction on the beach. She kept eating, desperately willing the food to give her an opportunity. It became quickly apparent that there was something not quite right about the flavor and it took all her willpower to swallow each bite. Dean followed suit and his expression soon mirrored Lydia's.

"This... duck, brings shame upon the duck community," he stated seriously.

Lydia and Dean soon broke into fits of laughter as they traded insults about the bird in question.

"It's a disaster of a duck," Lydia offered timidly.

Dean drove an accusatory finger into a piece of duck meat, "It doesn't deserve to be called a duck. Look at you, lying there, making me look bad in front of our guest. You street pigeon!" he said melodramatically.

"I'm sorry it didn't work out, Dean. I appreciate all the trouble you went to," offered Lydia.

"Do *not* finish that monstrosity," commanded Dean, "I'll call for pizza."

Lydia stood up suddenly, "I'm sorry about earlier," she blurted.

"Don't be sorry. I read the moment wrong, it was my fault," responded Dean.

"No, it wasn't that. I was... I wasn't expecting. Dammit, why can't I say what I mean!" Lydia erupted.

Dean waved a hand, "You don't have to-"

"My ex was... not a great person, as I think you've worked out. I came here to get away from that. I didn't expect to feel anything for anyone, not so quickly anyway."

Dean nodded soberly, "It's okay. You don't have to explain yourself to me. Come on, might be best if we get you home, eh?" he said with gentle resignation.

Lydia traipsed toward Dean slowly and deliberately; she draped her arms around his neck, "Later," she said in a whisper.

She kissed him softly, her body rising up to meet his. The sensation of his lips on hers was intoxicating. Lydia felt as though she couldn't get close enough to the warmth of Dean's body. His strong arms engulfed her smaller frame. Lydia felt an overwhelming desire to disappear into the man, as though he were a portal to some far-off place. Dean ran a calloused hand down Lydia's side, over her hip, to her thigh and back up under her dress. Lydia moaned, an exhalation of release, a sound of intense pressure melting away. She pushed forward and haphazardly lead Dean to the bedroom. When their forward momentum was stopped by Dean's big, wooden bed, she pushed him onto the mattress with one purposeful shove. She climbed on top of him and Dean's hands traced the shape of her. Lydia felt an irresistible shudder move through her body, as they began to move together as one.

KITTY'S SKIN BRISTLED as Mason moved close, too close. Her eyes kept darting between the man's crazed face and the broken latch on the front door. Had anyone heard the ruckus? Maybe someone called the cops, even if it was a noise complaint, that would do.

"Where the hell did she go? You two are thick as thieves. She tells you everything, you little gossipy whore!" Mason screamed into Kitty's face.

Why had she come home today of all days? She had been smart enough to stay at Donna's house, just like Lydia had told her to; she just didn't want to feel like she was imposing. She was careful not to tell Donna too much about Lydia's escape plans. Maybe Donna would have understood. Lydia had stayed there after Mason had beaten her so badly, it looked like she had gone into anaphylaxis or something. Mason probably would have twigged and stormed over to Donna's at some point anyway; she was Lydia's boss after all.

"I d-don't know, I've told you a-already!" yelled Kitty, exasperated.

"I'll crush you like an insect, you know I will!"

Mason wrapped his long fingers around Kitty's slender neck, as he ground her into the wall like he was trying to squash her out of existence. He choked her until she thought she might pass out, then, without warning he let go altogether. Smiling darkly, he said, "You don't want me to pay a visit to your dear old mom, do you?"

"D-Don't you dare-" began Kitty.

"Well tell me where your bitch of a sister is and I won't have to," interjected Mason. Kitty looked at her feet then back up at Mason, then she told him everything he wanted to know.

LYDIA WOKE TO A SOFT kiss on her forehead; she opened her eyes dreamily and saw a familiar face. The dark hair and eyes that she knew so well, the thick beard; it was Mason's face! She jumped up and out of the bed, blood pulsing like a jack-hammer in her head.

"Is my duck-breath that bad?" asked Dean jokingly.

"Y-Yeah, Oh God!" replied Lydia doubled over.

"I better give the fangs another brush then," said Dean, scooping Lydia up in a hardy embrace.

He kissed her passionately and Lydia's fear drained away. There was little respite from the relentless questions echoing through her mind, but the events of the week had made Lydia feel lost, in the best sense of the word. There was almost too much to process and she was forced to simply go with the current.

"Are you happy with cereal for breakfast? Promise I won't muck it up," Dean offered.

"Sounds good to me. Mind if I use your shower?"

"Knock yourself out."

Lydia fiddled with the hot and cold-water knobs, until she found a comfortable temperature. Dean's showerhead was twice the size of the one at her house and the pressure was incredible. She worked up a soapy lather in her hands and ran them all over her body. Dean's face crept into her thoughts as she touched herself. She closed her eyes and let the water massage her neck and shoulders, losing herself in the moment. From behind her, big hands slid up over her hips and Dean's lips found the back of her neck.

"Touch me," Lydia cooed.

Dean ran his hands over Lydia's breasts, his fingers cascading over her nipples. He moved his palms over her sternum, her stomach and down between her legs. Her knees buckled, as he stroked her, explored her with fingers, that seemed to know exactly what she wanted. Lydia spun around and kissed Dean's chest; he wrapped his hands around her thighs and hoisted her up, so that they were face to face. In that moment, Lydia felt an aching need like nothing she had ever experienced; she arched her back and Dean was inside of her. Lydia imagined her cells were exploding all at once and for the first time, in a long time, she felt like everything was going to be okay.

THEY MADE LOVE SPORADICALLY until sundown, stopping only to rehydrate, or eat their way through Dean's dwindling cereal stores. Every so often, Dean would study Lydia's face, examining her as though she was something rare, exotic and surprising. Lydia watched Dean as he did things, smiling like she used to on Christmas mornings, as a child. She remembered how weird she thought Dean had been for doing the same thing, only days ago. She'd come a long way.

"In the interest of our digestive health, I'm going to suggest we go out for dinner," Dean said on the spur of the moment, with his trademark smile.

"Can't argue there, hot stuff," replied Lydia.

"Hot stuff?" questioned Dean.

"Yeah, I regretted that one as soon as it came out my mouth," replied Lydia.

Lydia insisted that they stop off at her place so she could grab a change of clothes. She chose a summery, linen dress with spaghetti straps, the kind that was normally worn over a top that would cover her arms. Lydia tried it on its own and the dress looked so much better and felt so much cooler without the extra layers. She looked at her yellowing bruises in the mirror and for a moment she almost fell into old habits. Without giving herself more time to second-guess things, Lydia breezed out the front door. Dean remained silent as she climbed into the truck, but Lydia thought she could see the beginnings of an approving look from the corner of her eye.

They parked the vehicle back at Dean's place and he suggested they walk to his local dinner haunt. Before they set off, Dean pulled Lydia close to him, "You're beautiful," he whispered before kissing her gently. Lydia could feel the warmth of tears welling in her eyes. They strolled hand in hand for several blocks and Lydia waited for some kind of awkward tension or embarrassment, but it never came. She felt more natural being in Dean's presence, than she ever had with Mason. Mason. Why did he have to haunt her; couldn't she just exorcise him from her psyche once and for all. He was no longer welcome.

Lydia and Dean exchanged rough sketches of their respective backstories as they walked. Dean spoke of a respectable, working class family life, one that was tempered with the torment of being bullied relentlessly at school. His teen years soon became all about survival and asserting his masculinity by fighting or being crazier than his peers.

Lydia opened up about her childhood. Her family had lived on an acreage and she had whiled away her free time wandering her world and trying in vain to capture it on paper. She divulged the fact that she came a hair's breadth away from being called Iris, even though she loved the flower of the same name. She had her father to thank for naming her after her paternal grandmother. Yet her father was a strict disciplinarian and so her mother became her shelter. She and her younger sister would run away from home, at least once a month. Lydia would pack cheese, bread, milk and cookies into a little case and sit around waiting for the opportune time to make a break for it. Inevitably, Kitty would see her and beg to come along. The pair of them would only make it to the fence line of the property, before they missed Mom too much to carry on. Kitty. Lydia hoped she was okay; she hoped she was safe.

"We're here: my favorite seafood restaurant on the coast. It's my favorite cos' it's the closest," announced Dean.

The place was longer than it was wide and an array of coast-dwellers and tourists swirled glasses of white wine, scraped utensils on plates and studied other patrons. The walls were lightly colored and the room felt airier and more spacious than it really was. Small, agile, sunny-looking waitresses whizzed through the space wearing black t-shirts and mini-skirts. Maybe that's what Dean really came for; those skirts left little to the imagination. They sat at an outdoor table and ordered combinations of local seafood that Dean had promised to be some of the best in the country. The service was prompt and the food didn't disappoint. For dessert, they ordered a platter of tropical fruit, some that Lydia had never seen before.

"Dean... what on earth is that?" Lydia asked, pointing to a small, green, apple-like fruit that looked drab next to its brightly colored companions.

"That, my lady, is a black capote," offered Dean.

"Isn't he the author of Breakfast at Tiffany's?" laughed Lydia.

"Well, he's also delicious. Here, try some," said Dean, cutting round the skin, to reveal dark, brown flesh. Scooping some out with a spoon, he popped it into Lydia's mouth before she could protest.

She thought for a moment, "Mmmm! It tastes like... chocolate pudding!" she yelled excitedly.

"That's why it's referred to around here as: chocolate pudding fruit," said Dean, one eyebrow cocked.

"What other surprises do you have in store for me?"

"Well, there's a fish that makes its home in the waters of the Great Barrier Reef that tastes exactly like roast lamb," he stated.

"Really?" Lydia shot back.

"No," Dean retorted.

The pair laughed as they tucked into their food. Dean fed Lydia all the exotic fruit she could handle and before long they'd finished just about everything. They were preparing to leave when a large dull-eyed twenty-something year old male and his lank-haired friend, approached the table. They weren't even patrons of the restaurant; the two young men looked like they had been drinking in a park somewhere.

Dull-eyes leant heavily on Lydia and Dean's table, "Whoa, dude! You really like beating on your missus, don't you matey," he said, staring and pointing at Lydia's bruising. He said it loudly enough so that most of the restaurant patrons heard and began whispering to one another.

"What did you say to me?" Dean growled, standing up to stare the twenty-something in the eye, before Lydia shot him a 'please don't' look.

"He's sayin' that she's a fine lookin' woman and maybe she don't like being belted," offered lank-hair.

"You don't know what you're talking about, either of you. Just leave, we don't want a whole thing here, okay?" said Dean through gritted teeth, gripping the table so tight, his knuckles were whitening.

Dull-eyes pointed an outstretched thumb at Dean, "Hey, look, old punchy here's getting upset," he announced.

"Yeah, don't want to get belted by a senior citizen, eh?" lank-hair chimed in.

"Look, Dean's not like that, okay guys?" pleaded Lydia, her voice quavering.

"Oh, Dean! That's a pretty name for your ass-faced boyfriend, isn't it?" lank-hair said mockingly, as he placed a hand on each of Lydia's shoulders, massaging her with dirt-encrusted fingers.

Dean threw his chair back and rose to his feet, "Hands off, idiot!" he spat.

"Maybe you'd better piss off home, Deany-boy," oozed dull-eyes, placing the flat of his hand on Dean's chest.

"Be careful, man. His tee has a Harley on it. He's probably a 'Hell's Demon' or some crap," said lank-hair.

Dean grabbed dull-eye's hand so hard, it made the younger man squeak; Dean yanked his arm, simultaneously punching him in the face. Dull-eyes sank to his knees as lank-hair rounded the table and came at Dean. Dean moved on him before lank-hair had a chance to think; he kicked a foot out from under him and landed a quick jab to his throat. Dull-eyes had recovered enough to charge his considerable bulk in Dean's direction. Dean waited until the last minute and side-stepped his assailant, pushing him forward and down, into the concrete sidewalk with his own momentum.

Dean grabbed Lydia's hand and briskly led her away from the restaurant. They had walked less than a block when Lydia dug in her heels and pulled her hand from Dean's grasp.

"What's wrong?" Dean asked.

"What's wrong?" Lydia repeated.

Dean pointed back toward the restaurant, "Those guys? You're going to stick up for them? They're stoners with something to prove," he spat.

"Why is violence always the damn answer?" Lydia found herself yelling.

"I know it bloody isn't, okay. I know that better than anyone. You can't let people just walk all over you, though, Lydia. Sometimes, it's about protecting you and yours."

"Oh. 'Yours'?" Lydia questioned incredulously.

"I think you know what I meant," began Dean, pausing to collect his thoughts. "I'm sorry, it's the adrenaline talking."

"It's like a drug, isn't it?" asked Lydia sadly. She turned and walked away; she couldn't look at him anymore. There was a feeling of foreboding in her belly, like a seismic vibration that was shaking her world apart. Violence could no longer be a part of her life if she was to heal.

DORA WASN'T HOME WHEN Lydia decided to lob up on her doorstep. It had taken the better part of an hour to find the place, as her phone's map app kept sending her in the wrong direction. She walked her tired feet around back and took a seat on a garden bench under a beautiful, old fig tree. The moon was peeking through the branches and fruit-bats screeched and ate things from the trees at the far end of the yard. She couldn't help but go over and over the evening's events in her mind. Had she overreacted? No, she had no room in her life for more brutality. Wasn't he just trying to protect her? It soon seemed clear to Lydia that she had rushed into things with Dean way too quickly; he was a rebound guy and that was that. She needed to survive on her own, build her own strengths. She had made it this far on her own and this new home of hers was meant to be a sanctuary, not a battleground.

"Oh, hi Petal! I saw the side gate was open and I thought it was those bloody neighbor kids! Come to absorb the sage counsel of your personal oracle, have you?" Dora said as she breezed through the yard, hurtling toward Lydia.

"I-I guess," replied Lydia.

"Come on, let's get inside and get some peppermint tea into you. Maybe something stronger?"

"No. Tea sounds great," Lydia responded.

"The something stronger will be for me then, pet. Hell of a day. I told a client that her brat of a child wasn't too bright and that it would need some remedial schooling unless she wanted it suckling at her teat well into its thirties and she storms away from the stall without paying! That's gratitude for you!"

Lydia marveled at the way her friend could both speak her mind no matter the outcome and fire off long sentences without taking a breath. They entered Dora's home through the rear door into a kitchen that was large enough for a dining setting. There were drying herbs hanging from racks on the wall and reliefs of the sun, moon and stars displayed above the old, woodfire stove. There were shelves and shelves of bottled ingredients and an array of what looked like very old cookbooks. A spider had made its web in the corner of the room, with a whole pantry worth of web-wrapped insects in it; Dora was the live and let live type. A print of 'Witches Sabbath' by Goya, hung ominously above the doorway into the living room area. Lydia could see shadows dancing under the painting and two sleek, black cats bounded into the room from the front of the house. They began to mewl frantically at the return of their mistress.

Dora dropped down to stroke her pets. "This is Romulus and Remus. Boys, this is Lydia: Mumma's best friend," she said to the cats, without a hint of irony.

"Nice to meet you," said Lydia to the animals, as though it was the most natural thing in the world. "They're very handsome."

"They're wicked! A little wickedness makes for a happy home, if you ask me," Dora quipped.

The house felt inviting but strange; It was like there were different rules inside the walls of the mysterious building. Curtains, hanging in front of closed windows, danced in non-existent wind. Floorboards creaked, as though something heavy lurked around, unseen. There was a sound, like breathing, that would stop abruptly, when Lydia strained to hear it. There was a scent in the air, a blend of exotic ingredients, oils and incense, as well as something inexplicable. The cats seemed to sense Lydia's mild alarm and rubbed themselves against her affectionately, vibrating with purrs and weaving their silky bodies between her legs in figure-eight formation.

"Well, the two house-guardians have accepted you. You're a denizen of the place now, Lyds," said Dora as she busied herself pouring boiling water and arranging mugs.

She brought the tea things over to the dining table on a wooden tray, carved with forest animals. Lydia sat down and looked through the ivy laden window, at the yard outside; there were brightly colored birds out there now, frolicking in a stone bird bath. Fat, black lizards darted this way and that, on the window sill and luminous butterflies, fluttered about.

"This is a beautiful place, Dor," complimented Lydia.

"Did you expect anything less?" said Dora with a wicked grin, as she poured tea for Lydia, then herself.

"Actually. I half expected you to live in an elaborate tree-house, or something magical like that," replied Lydia.

"Well, gotta' keep up the air of mystique. I don't want to deliver what people expect," added Dora, looking deeply into Lydia's eyes.

"You know why I'm here, don't you?" said Lydia.

"Something happened with our outlaw, didn't it?"

Lydia traced the lip of her cup with her finger, "Yeah, it did.'"

"Well, you tell aunty Dora all about it. I could tell you needed to vent as soon as I saw you. Looked like a pot-belly stove about to blow, you did," added Dora, tipping whiskey into her cup from a small, hip-flask, engraved with a pentacle.

"Not keen on the 'pot-belly' bit but okay. Dean and I... well we sort of hooked up a little bit," confessed Lydia.

"Hooked up? What, are you thirteen?" asked Dora playfully.

Lydia tilted her head, "Don't make this any harder than it is, spooky lady. Anyway, it's serious."

Dora pressed her fingers to both temples, "First tell me this: are those buns as tight as I imagined?"

"Dora!"

"Okay, okay. A single lady can dream. Go on," said Dora, switching to a tone of seriousness.

"Well, it was fine, that is until these guys started a whole thing and then he punched them and-"

Dora interrupted, "Wowee! He hit some guys? Defending your honor, I bet!"

"No! Well, sort of. I don't know," stammered Lydia, taking a sip of tea to calm her nerves.

"Oh, brought some bad stuff back up, did it?" asked Dora.

"Sure did," replied Lydia.

"You know I don't get that vibe from him though, don't you? I think you and he are similar in a lot of ways, the ways that count anyway. In my humble opinion, pet, it pays to stay open to what the Goddess offers. We're just stardust, shaped into castles and slowly eroding on the shores of time."

Lydia grinned, "That's beautiful. You should write a book."

"Nah, love. I'm more of a reader. Plus, I don't have that level of commitment. Anyway, this is not about me, petal. Can you not chalk up Dean's one-off act of violence to protectiveness? There's a tidal wave of sadness and pain out there for each and every one of us. There are people who want to do us harm in all sorts of terrible ways. But the beauty of those experiences is that they can hone our instincts and give us the ability to avoid them in the future. You just need to make sure those instincts are pointed in the right direction. Embrace the good stuff, Lyds and I really feel positive that Dean is the good stuff. Hold the positive things close, it's the only way to counteract all the poisonous crap."

"You're probably right, you usually are. It's just that when I saw him beating on those guys, it made me feel terrified and sick," said Lydia, looking out the window.

Dora reached across the table and gripped Lydia's hand tightly, "Shouldn't you maybe be telling *him* this, love?" she said gently.

DEAN HAD SPENT AN HOUR driving around looking for Lydia; he had dropped in at her place, but to no avail. He was a little annoyed with her and her reaction to what had happened at the restaurant. After going over the whole scene in his head, he still felt justified in his response to the situation. What kind of guy was he, if he let random idiots put their hands on a woman like that? He would have had a hard time respecting himself if he had just walked away. Gang fights had taught him that about himself; it was about honor and courage, in its purest form. If he could just talk to Lydia and explain how he felt, he was sure she would understand. He was never one to make excuses for his behavior, but he wanted, needed, Lydia to know him, as well as anyone could be known.

Dean found a parking space and pulled up at The Esplanade, opposite the ocean. He sat for a while before jumping out of his truck and shuffling toward the beach. He took off his boots and wandered the sand forlornly; he couldn't help but notice the laughter of nearby happy couples. There were people walking hand in hand, on after-dinner strolls, or just enjoying the cool of the ocean-spray. When he was with the gang, he attracted a very specific kind of woman; they seemed to like the idea of him, more than the real thing. He had never really met anyone quite like Lydia and now he'd gone and lost her. The relentless sound of waves crashing soothed him somewhat, but his mind still raced; that was until an unwanted distraction dropped into his line of vision.

He had to look twice to confirm who it was that he had just seen. The blonde goatee beard, the long unwashed hair and the dubious posture. It was the man whose parents had optimistically named: Thomas James Wilcott; the world at large knew him by his gang-given nickname: Knuckles. Knuckles was meandering about, drinking liquor from a bottle concealed in brown paper and pestering passing women. Any turbulence from angry partners, was met with a raised fist. Knuckles certainly wasn't the kind of man to be tangled with. There was a story floating around about Knuckles beating his own brother to death, with a cricket bat, over a money dispute. No one had the guts to ask the guy about his brother. Dean, after processing the initial shock, meditated on how little had changed. The people he used to run with didn't seem to want anything better for themselves and they certainly wouldn't empathize with him. He'd crawled his way out of the depths of some stagnant water and there was no way he would ever go back.

Dean decided to make himself scarce; the last thing he needed was Knuckles making a scene or worse yet: telling the rest of the guys that he'd been spotted. He quickly put his boots back on and made for the sidewalk, stealthily moving toward the cover of a nearby toilet block. Dean had just made it inside, when he heard a gravelly voice that made the hairs on the back of his neck stand to attention.

"Dean-o! Where ya' been, mate? Ya' got no time for yer' brothers no more?" shouted Knuckles.

"Knuck. How are you?" Dean shot back, spinning around and trying to look unflustered.

"Mate, Brando and the mob haven't been the same since ya' took off. You comin' back soon? We've got a little jobbie for ya' mate," Knuckles said, slapping Dean hard on the arm.

"Mate, I'm takin' some time for me'self. I need to sort me head out," replied Dean, falling into rhythm with Knuckle's mode of speaking.

"Yer' not grassing on yer mates are ya', Deano. I know that Donk shot ya', he's been telling everyone about it. He had it in his stupid head that ya' wanted to ditch the Colonial Boys. But ya' wouldn't do that, would ya' mate?" said Knuckles, his Neanderthal brow furrowing, reducing his eyes to coin-slots.

"C'mon, Knuck. I'm no squealer. Tell Donk: no 'ard feelings, yeah? And tell Brando, I'll see him sometime soon, alright mate?" Dean retorted.

Knuckles folded his arms across his barrel chest, "When?"

"Soon," responded Dean.

Knuckles stepped forward, looming over Dean, "When soon?"

"Soon mate. C'mon, let me buy ya' a beer."

Knuckles pulled a knife concealed in his belt buckle and proceeded to pick his smoke-stained teeth with it, "We don't want bloody beer from ya', mate. We want loyalty. Otherwise Donk might have to finish what he started." he rumbled.

Dean's hands clenched into fists at his side and his core muscles tightened, bracing for a fight. His thoughts then turned to Lydia and the look of disappointment on her face after the dinner incident. His hands relaxed.

"Alright, Knuck. I hear ya'. I'll pay youse a visit as soon as possible," Dean lied.

"Cos' that missus I seen ya' wiv', the one with the nice mouth, I reckon the boys would like to get to know her too," said Knuckles greasily, squeezing his crotch with ringed fingers.

Dean swallowed his rage down, hard. He could feel the cortisol pumping through his body, readying him for the salvo of punches he desperately wanted to rain on his former friend. He envisioned Knuckles watching his house, seeing him with Lydia. Dean mentally berated himself for not being more observant; he was never that clumsy. He would check Lydia's house again to be safe; if they'd followed them that far, who knows what they'd do. At this stage, they just wanted him back. Threats were being thrown around so they were still in the bargaining phase; that's why Knuckles was talking and not beating. Dean had seen it all before; he would just have to stay calm a little longer, for his and Lydia's sake now.

"Her? She's a little piece I've been killing time with. She's nobody. Anyway, I'll be around soon. Ya' got my word," said Dean with a dead calm that came out of necessity.

"Ya' better," said Knuckles icily.

Knuckles turned and walked away slowly and Dean wondered whether the man had believed his lies about Lydia. He didn't want her stained by his former life; he wanted to protect her from it. Maybe the best thing was to leave her alone completely; it seemed as though that's what she wanted anyway. If he could just find her and talk to her; but then again, what would he tell her? Would he tell her there was a large group of gangsters who had now identified her as a bargaining chip? She didn't need the additional stress on top of everything she was dealing with. He would look out for her, if she would let him.

Dean walked for hours. His feet were throbbing by the time the sun peeked over the horizon. Surfers Paradise was only ever devoid of people in the wee hours of the morning, for a short while. The cawing of seagulls fighting over scraps, echoed through the empty streets. Dean had stopped into an all-night tobacconist and bought cigarettes. He pulled one out and lit it with a cheap, plastic lighter. He hadn't smoked in several years, but he certainly wasn't feeling himself. The first drag made Dean's head spin. It dawned on him that even though he'd left the gang, he couldn't step out of himself. He had dreams of living a peaceful life and that peaceful life included someone that he could love and protect. Surely that wasn't a bad thing to want. Every face Dean saw soon became Lydia's face and every laugh he heard was her laugh. He threw the cigarettes in the trash and thought about heading off.

It hit Dean then that he didn't know the woman that well; he hadn't the first idea where to find her. He didn't know where her friend with the red hair lived. Dora, that was it; he remembered her saying that she worked at the night markets, but they had well and truly closed, many hours ago. Either way, stalking a woman wasn't his bag. Dean allowed the memory of Lydia to permeate his thoughts for a moment. He loved the way she looked at him, as though she was strangely excited by him despite, her best intentions. He loved her shiny, brown hair and the way her laughter erupted out of her, like it came as a surprise to no one more than herself. She'd felt good in his arms; she'd felt right. It dawned on Dean then, that maybe he did know Lydia and he knew exactly what to do next.

MASON'S PLANE TOUCHED down not a moment too soon. The woman next to him was working on his last nerve. She had been in the seat behind him all the way from Denver to Brisbane and now she was on his connecting flight as well. Not only was she an incessant talker, but when her ugly baby wasn't wriggling or crying, it was staring at Mason, with its big, stupid eyes. Mason stroked his beard, as he always did when irritated. He hated children, but babies most of all. He was convinced they had nothing articulate to say due to a lack of ambition. Lydia had talked about wanting one of those creatures when they had first started dating; what a ridiculous notion.

The baby's mother had red hair; he'd always hated red hair. Then an image popped into Mason's mind: a redhead that he'd met at the store where Lydia worked. Lydia had already left work for home, when he rocked up at the store. He liked to surprise her with the odd spot-check, see if she was behaving like a tramp in front of other men. The redhead was about five-foot something, pretty short, Mason remembered. She looked like some fortune-teller or something and she had an accent. At first Mason had figured her for British. She might have been Australian, now that he thought about it. What was her name? Donna? Doreen? How had he been so stupid? That redhead must have helped her move all the way to the Southern Hemisphere. He imagined wringing the little redhead's neck.

Mason threw off his safety belt well before the plane had finished taxiing; he was the first one up and rummaging through the overhead locker, when a female flight attendant approached him.

"You'll have to take your seat until the Captain has turned off the seatbelt sign, sir," she said with a honeyed voice laced with ire.

Mason employed every ounce of self-control he had; he wanted nothing more than to punch the uniformed woman in the face. Getting arrested would have halted his progress in finding Lydia, though and he had to make sure he stayed off the police radar until then.

"So sorry. Just a little eager to get out and explore your beautiful Gold Coast," Mason oozed.

"Oh, where are you travelling from originally?" asked the flight attendant cheerily, as Mason obediently sat back down.

"Uh… Michigan," lied Mason. Reassessing the woman in front of him, now so much more appealing after her change of attitude. She had shapely breasts under that uniform and a sexy glint in her eye.

"Oh, nice. I have friends out your way," she purred, staring at Mason's muscled arms.

"You get out there yourself?" asked Mason as he eyed her up and down once more.

Mason could feel the ugly baby's mother making judgmental faces that he cared nothing about. Maybe he could screw this uniformed piece by way of compensation for having to fly all the way down under. The flight attendant droned on and on, but Mason had tuned out. He was lost in visions of naked, writhing flesh. Then, suddenly, Lydia's face emerged and with it, his nagging need for vengeance.

Finally, the time had come to disembark and Mason gave 'nice-breasts' his phone number. He powered through the terminal, whistling The Marriage of Figaro, as he made his way out onto the road. Stealing a taxi from an elderly man, he realized he wasn't exactly sure where he was headed. That silly cow of a sister had given him a vague idea, but he would have to do a fair bit of leg work to find his lost little lamb. Luckily money wasn't a problem and he worked for himself, so his time was his own. He would be a patient hunter and he would enjoy taking down his prey all the more for the effort.

Chapter Five

The Hunted

Lydia dragged her feet back to her house. The morning air was cool as the heat of the day hadn't ramped up to full strength just yet. Her back was a little sore after sleeping on Dora's sofa. The sofa was fairly comfortable, but the black cats had slept on her all night and she hadn't moved a muscle for fear of disturbing them. Not that she'd slept right through anyway; in addition to the cacophony of strange nocturnal noises in Dora's house, Lydia had lay awake pondering her time with Dean. She had tried to convince herself that ending things with Dean, before they really started, was for the best. An older couple, walking hand in hand, passed Lydia on the sidewalk. Her heart ached a little at seeing two people who had probably been together for most of their lives, still expressing their affection for one another. Dora's advice echoed through her mind. Lydia pinched the bridge of her nose with her fingers; she needed to focus on practical things, like getting herself a job. The money she had squirreled away would run out soon. Dora was clear that she wouldn't be expecting rent money until Lydia found work; it gnawed at Lydia and she felt like she was taking advantage of her friend's kindness. Kitty had even covertly slipped a wad of cash in Lydia's pocket when they had last met; fancy her younger sister trying to take care of her older sibling.

"Ms. Hawkins, how are things?" came a deep voice from out of the ether. Lydia spun around to find Officer Barnes in full uniform, ambling toward her on the sidewalk.

"Oh, I'm fine Officer. What brings you this way?" Lydia responded.

"Just chatting to a couple of the neighbors about your prowler from the other night, in fact. We got a call from someone who said they saw a strange character stumbling around, on the very night you reported one. Older woman called it in, a little skittish though, so she didn't call right away. Terrible thing."

Lydia sighed, "What is?"

"Fear. On the one hand it stops us doing stupid things, on the other... it can be life threatening," said Officer Barnes gravely.

"Oh, I know. That's why I try to live as fearlessly as possible," Lydia lied.

"You know, I knew a woman, same age as you are now. She was being abused by her spouse for years and everyone around her knew it. No one reported it cos' people felt like that was butting in, back in those days. She didn't actually tell anyone about it, cos' she was terrified of what would happen. Well, what *did* happen was this: she was bloody beaten to death by that prick, before he was finally put away. Guess you could say that fear killed that young woman."

"You'll probably never know the fear she lived with, Officer," shot Lydia, wrapping her arms around herself. She was suddenly painfully aware, that her bruises were visible in the summer dress she still wore.

"No, I guess not. I'm certainly not judging her, Ms. Hawkins. Just laying down the facts."

"Okay, well that neighbor lady finally called you so then I guess she fought her fear and won. Is that the moral of all this?" said Lydia, a little annoyed.

"You can talk to me anytime, I guess that's the point," said Officer Barnes coolly.

"Well, I have nothing to add, I'm afraid."

"Okay. You have a good day. You know, gets to be that the longer you do this job, the better you can read people. Their past, their experiences, are like a story, right there on their face."

"Maybe some of those stories a-aren't for you to read." Lydia countered.

"Maybe. See you later, Ms. Hawkins," said Officer Barnes walking to his car.

Lydia looked at her feet as the man drove away. She didn't like being lectured and she certainly didn't like the idea of being 'read'. How many other people could read her like Brian Barnes? Maybe she wasn't as safe as she wanted to believe. Why couldn't people let her be someone new? Why keep dragging her back to her old life?

As she climbed the stairs to the front door, Lydia caught sight of something unexpected but familiar: it was the wooden chair she had admired at Dean's workshop. On the seat was a note that read: 'More bespoke furniture available, by request. P.S. Hope it's not crossing a line, but I threw in some flowers you might like, in your front yard, D'. Lydia looked at the previously empty flower beds that were now alive with freshly planted irises. Lydia felt a lump in her throat; she unlocked the door and managed to awkwardly carry the chair down the hall.

She stood admiring her gift for mere minutes before a loud rumbling outside caught her attention.

Lydia padded up the hallway to the open door and peered outside. There was Dean, astride a large, shiny motorbike, revving the engine and smiling contentedly at her. She paused for a moment; the skin on the back of her neck tingled and her heartbeat quickened. He was wearing a beaten-up brown, leather riding jacket and wrap-around sunglasses. She felt a heated attraction to the man that seemed to have intensified, during their brief parting. Lydia realized then, that she was weary of being scared; shivering and stuttering just solidified the 'little lamb' persona that Mason had lumped her with.

She ran down the stairs, bolted across to the bike and jumped on the back. Dean twisted around and pointed at the helmet atop a pannier bag behind Lydia and she put it on. He pulled her hands into position around his waist and Lydia held on tightly. Dean was relieved to find Lydia and her home unassailed. He would take her away, even for just a short while, somewhere they could find respite from the negative forces that meant them harm. On the road, he could really think. Maybe by the time they returned, he'd have come up with a course of action. Dean u-turned in the front yard, took a left onto the street and accelerated toward the hinterland. Lydia loved the thundering of the engine and the wind on her skin; the speed of the bike was jarring until she gave in to it. Caution quickly gave way to excitement and Lydia let out a scream of elation.

They roared past the dwindling suburban landscape that gave way to farms and then the rise into the rainforest. The air cooled suddenly as they were enveloped by verdant foliage and a vast canopy of tree limbs that formed a natural arbor over the road. The air was humid and alive. Flocks of parrots squawked and took to the air as the bike approached. There were falls here and there, casting water-spray rainbows and in places, fingers of light cascading through the trees onto the path ahead. After the bike had chewed through a good few miles, Dean suddenly hit the left indicator and they turned off the main road. A lush vista of hills and vegetation opened up before the pair, as they pulled up at a lookout. Lydia hopped off the bike and threw off her helmet, running to the fence-line to take in the bewitching scene. Dean followed her and wrapped his arms around her from behind; she had never felt so safe.

"I've never told anyone what I'm about to tell you," began Dean, after a while. "My Mum wasn't like other mums when I was growing up. She was a working girl."

"As in…" Lydia's voice trailed off.

"Yeah. She sold herself, starting from a young age. She was kicked outta' home by her religious parents. She questioned their beliefs and finally rejected them at about sixteen years of age. They were part of a cult, one of those ones where they come to your door with those magazines. They shunned her from their faith and never contacted her again. So, she was alone and the only way she could make enough money to live, was through street-walking. Before long she got into trouble. She accidentally got pregnant, with twins and she didn't know what to do. My Dad was one of her regular clients back then, but he'd been in love with her from the first time they'd been together. He offered to take her away and look after her and the babies. She refused at first, but the living and working in a crappy apartment with two kids screaming their heads off the whole time, eventually wore her down. Some of the johns would be so dissatisfied that they'd hit her. Sometimes she'd buy drugs off them so she could escape her life. Ultimately. My Dad won her over and the rest is history. He was never our biological Dad; I reminded him of that constantly. Anyway, now you know."

"Dean, I don't know what to say. Thank you for sharing that with me. I mean that," Lydia said warmly.

"I trust you. I'm not telling you to explain why I do things the way I do, or anything like that. I just wanted you to know where I came from, because it's the truth," Dean responded.

Lydia turned to face Dean, "My childhood was good, I think. My Dad was really tough and sort of... inaccessible, I suppose. When I left high-school, I worked for this stationary supply place in town. Mas-, I mean: my ex, would come in and flirt shamelessly with the other girls who worked there. I thought he was too handsome and too confident for someone like me, so I tried to avoid him. I think he started to zero in on me, because I seemed unavailable. So, he started pursuing me relentlessly. At first, I thought he was just a leader-type, like an alpha-male. Looking back now, it's pretty clear that he was domineering and pretty aggressive, even then. I caved in at some point and we started dating and for a while it was okay. I must have fallen in love with him somewhere along the way, or at least thought that I had. I relied on him so much and he seemed to get off on that. Soon he was telling me what to wear and what to eat and drink and do. He was always lording things over me; telling me I was uncultured and uneducated.

One day, when I was staying over at his house, I dropped something, a bowl or plate and he hit the roof. He started smashing dishes and glasses and pictures. Then he slapped me. He was shocked the first time and he apologized for days afterward. He cried one night and told me how much he loved me and that the last thing he ever wanted to do was hurt me. I even felt sorry for him, he seemed so remorseful, but he hit me again and again. Slapping turned into punching and somehow, I felt like it was because of something missing in me, something I had done wrong to make him what he was. When he would feel bad about everything, I really believed he could get better. I had to believe that. Deep down, I thought that if I could be better, then he could. T-that's all I can say about it," Lydia's voice started to break and Dean held her so close that she could feel his heartbeat.

The wind howled through the hills and a conspiracy of ravens flew past; their mournful cries echoing through the trees.

MASON HELD OUT HIS phone; on it was the last picture he'd ever taken of Lydia. She was wearing jeans and a loose top; the kind of attire that had become her uniform. Her hair was pulled back and she smiled in that forced, sort of pinched way that made Mason feel guilty, then agitated.

"No, mate. Never seen her," said the young man wearing a t-shirt with the words: 'Professional Muff Diver' on it. Mason stroked his beard so hard it hurt a little.

Mason had shown Lydia's picture to a dozen people in the center of Surfer's Paradise that morning. Kitty had confessed that Lydia was staying in a place not far from there, but she didn't know the exact address. Lydia hadn't told her, so that she would have the benefit of 'plausible deniability'; Mason believed her, but only after he'd broken Kitty's wrist. Stupid slut would really feel that on cold mornings.

No one had seen Lydia, or so they said. Mason thought about Lydia's redheaded Australian friend; he had a hard time remembering her in any sort of detail, she wasn't all that attractive. A description was of little use; Mason had seen at least a half-dozen women who fit the bill. No, the picture was his best bet. Maybe he would buy himself some different clothes; an outfit that made him look like a dumb-hick tourist. He dressed more stylishly than anyone in this paradise of surfers. His black, button-down shirt alone probably cost more than most of the simpletons he'd encountered made in a month. On the plus side, there were plenty of beautiful women around; they seemed to appreciate his powerful physique unlike, Lydia the runaway lamb. He wanted to punish her so much, that he could taste the rising bile in the back of his throat. She would wish she had never left him.

Mason walked into a store that sold surfing equipment and clothing. He bought some boardshorts, t-shirts, hats and sunglasses. He hazarded a visit to a local bottle shop and astoundingly, found a couple of semi-drinkable reds. He headed back to his ocean-front hotel to change and collect his thoughts over a glass of grenache-shiraz.

He entered his suite and immediately opened the glass balcony door, to let the sea-breeze in. The place was turning out to be more pleasant than he had expected; maybe he'd relocate once Lydia had been shown the true meaning of respect and submission. Lydia. Mason envisioned her by the hotel pool, wearing a bikini. She'd worn a bikini only one time for him, when he'd flown her to Hawaii for an impromptu vacay. She looked so good back then, before she got all modest on him. He suddenly felt a wave of lust that was exacerbated by his third glass of wine. Mason leafed through the travel brochures and local area guidebooks on the coffee table. He found what he needed and picked up the room phone and dialed.

"Hi, my name is... John," said Mason, cursing himself for not picking a better alias.

"Yes, John. How can we help you today?" came the breathy reply.

"I'd like a woman, mid-thirties, about five-ten, with dark brown hair and a slightly curvy build. Can you manage that?"

"Oh yes, handsome. I have just the lady." Mason bristled a little at the use of the word 'handsome'. How did she know? She happened to be right, but what a stupid assumption.

"I'll be needing an hour, I'm at the Paradise View Plaza."

"She'll be there in fifteen to twenty minutes. Be sure to have cash, or a valid credit card please John."

The escort arrived at the hotel foyer after three more glasses and the reception-desk called Mason on the phone to announce her. Mason buzzed her in and was surprised at how much she reminded him of Lydia, even though her facial features couldn't have been more different.

"Hi, lover. I'm Bethany," announced the escort as she breezed into the room.

"John," Mason said curtly, proffering a stack of cash. Mason poured the last glass of wine from the bottle and offered it to Bethany. It was mostly sediment anyway.

"Thanks, gorgeous. Straight to business, I like that in a man," purred Bethany.

Mason peeled off his clothes and headed into the bedroom, the escort following closely behind. She pulled open her handbag and produced a bottle of lubricant, a strip of condoms and her phone. She wrote a quick text and sent it. Mason knew that she was letting the agency know that everything was under control; he was well versed in the hiring and usage of hookers. Bethany had only started stroking Mason's chest, with her manicured fingers, when he broke away and made for his suitcase, in the room's built-in closet. Rustling around for a moment, he returned brandishing a red dress.

"Put this on," he instructed.

"Anything you say," Bethany said calmly. She shimmied into the dress and twirled for Mason's approval.

He stared at her with glassy eyes; stumbling toward Bethany, Mason seemed mesmerized. He cupped her face in his hands and then collapsed against her, inhaling the traces of Lydia's scent. Bethany looked about the room, unsure what to say.

"Lydia, I knew you'd end up back where you belong," Mason whispered.

"Oh, that's right John. It's me: Olivia," replied Bethany.

"What did you say?" spat Mason, pushing away from Bethany.

"Sorry?" said Bethany, taken aback.

Mason punched the wall, "You damned stupid bitch! Get out! Go on! You're nothing like her!" he screamed, tears streaming down his reddening face.

Bethany scooped up her things, "No refunds, you psycho!"

"Leave the dress!" Mason yelled sharply.

Bethany hurriedly changed her clothes and shakily fumbled around, trying to escape as quickly as possible. The door slammed and Mason slumped against the foot of the bed, sinking down to the floor. He pulled Lydia's dress off of the bed, where Bethany the hard of hearing hooker had dumped it. Cradling the still warm garment, he sobbed in bursts, convulsing as salty tears and snot snaked into his thick, dark beard.

LYDIA JUMPED OFF OF Dean's bike excitedly. She threw off her helmet, then hugged and kissed him. Dean ambled after Lydia as she barreled up the stairs and spilled into the house. He looked around for signs of intrusion, finding none, Dean sauntered down the hallway, still feeling tranquil after their excursion. He entered the kitchen to find Lydia, hunched over her phone and white as a sheet.

"What is it?" queried Dean

"I l-left my phone here. I didn't want to be d-disturbed... b-but, ummm," stuttered Lydia. Dean rubbed Lydia's back affectionately.

"It's okay," Dean said.

"Kitty - my sister - messaged me. It's my ex. H-He's coming." Lydia sobbed, falling into Dean's arms. Dean squeezed her tightly. Her body shuddered and Dean felt a swell of protective instinct.

"Let's get away from here. We'll just pack up my truck and leave. My sister has a place in the far north: a little place called Innisfail. We can stay there for the time being, until we work out what to do next," Dean said decisively.

"Dean, you don't have to get all caught up in my life," Lydia replied.

"Lydia. I don't feel obligated. I want to be with you. Your problems are my problems," Dean said, holding Lydia's face in his hands.

She could feel the roughness of his palms against the soft skin of her cheeks. He was strong, inside and out; that much was clear. Was he strong enough to stand with her against the large, angry skeleton in her closet?

"I've run to a whole new country and he still managed to track me down. I don't want to run anymore."

"Then we dig in and defend," said Dean, all grit and steely determination.

Dean grabbed Lydia's hand and the pair left Lydia's house for his bike once more. They rode down the highway and traversed several side-streets, until they came to a warehouse with a large target for a sign. They made their way inside and after a brief conversation with – and subsequent payment to - the stocky proprietor, Dean escorted Lydia onto a well-used shooting range.

"You want me to shoot a gun?" asked Lydia disbelievingly.

"Trust me," countered Dean.

"I've fired a rifle before, when I was younger. I was different then. I don't know if I can do this."

"Lydia Hawkins, you're capable and intelligent and cool as hell," replied Dean warmly.

"This is crazy," said Lydia, closing her eyes for a moment. "Right now, crazy's good."

"That's my girl."

An instructor showed Lydia how to lock and load several different handguns. Dean and Lydia took turns firing their respective weapons at paper targets, with varying degrees of success. Dean's approach was calm, measured and practiced; Lydia's was all nerves and dropped bullets.

Gradually, Lydia's apprehension subsided and she started to actually enjoy the distraction. When she landed her first near-bullseye, she screamed jubilantly and embraced Dean; even the taciturn instructor looked pleased. Dean encouraged Lydia to shoot more and more weapons as he saw her confidence grow. After a while, though, Lydia became withdrawn.

"You don't expect me to shoot *him*, do you?" Lydia questioned.

"I don't expect you to do anything. I just want you to find that inner badass; the one that I could see from day one," Dean asserted.

"You should probably never disagree with me then," Lydia joked, shaping her hand into a pretend gun and pointing it at Dean. She laughed.

"You know, if you you're not keen on shooting him, you can always punch him in the plums," Dean offered.

"The plums?" Lydia queried. Dean looked down, then up, then down again once more, pushing his crotch forward.

"Ohhhh, right," said Lydia, laughing.

"You're going to be okay, Lydia."

Chapter Six

Fight or Flight

The earth was moist and still warm, even after a dousing with the hose.

"Getting on with some planting, are we?" queried the Police Officer.

"Yeah, keeps me busy," Dean shot back, looking up slowly.

The Officer rested a hand on the painted wood of the front fence, "You the gardener, are you?"

Dean continued working. "You could say that."

"You work for the elderly chap that lives here, then," baited the Officer.

"Don't know any elderly bloke. He might be the previous tenant," said Dean quickly, as he smoothed out the earth around the iris plants.

The Policeman bent over the fence line, "Friend of Lydia's, is it?"

"Acquaintance, more like."

"You been acquainted with her long, then?" asked Officer Barnes, his words landing, like well-aimed blows.

"Not long. Look, can I help you with something, Officer?" asked Dean, his annoyance bubbling to the surface.

The Officer smiled, happy to have struck a chord, "I'm Officer Brian Barnes, son. Your name is?"

"D-Daniel. Daniel O'Connor," lied Dean, worried that he was being transparent.

"Well, Mr. O'Connor, I was going to ask the same of you. What you need to know about me is: I'm not ambitious. I'm not gunning to make

Detective. Truth is: not quick on my feet these days neither. One thing I am, though, is smart. Sharp as a razor blade, some say. So, let's leave the crap on the flowers and then maybe, I can help you."

Dean remembered the conversation with Officer Barnes earlier that day in vivid detail; the man came across as a hard-case, but underneath it all, Dean sensed strong, driving conviction. During his time with the gang, he'd come across the law more times than he could count. There was a variety of differing approaches; there were the cops that wanted to add notches to their belt and the ones who wanted the world to know how much they hated the criminal underworld. There were the green ones, who could be talked around and occasionally, the incompetents or the corrupt, who could be bamboozled or bargained with. But every so often, Dean would come across a career cop, one who recognized that yearning in Dean: the yearning to be free.

"Where are you?" asked Lydia, stroking hair from Dean's forehead.

"I say we just go. Get right away from them. Simple as that," Dean announced, snapping out of his reverie.

"Them?" repeated Lydia.

"Him, I meant. Let him run out of time and money and patience. He'll never find you at my sister's place."

"What if he does? You don't know my ex like I do. He gets... obsessed."

"Then we'll work it out together."

Dean held Lydia and then kissed her. She knew that he was right, deep down. She could dig her heels in all she wanted but, in the end, she feared the outcome. There always was that nagging question: would he kill her? Now she worried that Mason would go toe-to-toe with Dean and she knew that Dean wasn't the kind of man to back down. Would they kill each other? Leaving it all behind once again, distancing the both of them from Mason would be the only way to avoid that possibility.

"Come on, pack some things. You should call Dora later and tell her you'll be leaving, but don't tell anyone where we're headed, yeah?"

"Okay," returned Lydia resignedly.

MASON'S HIRE CAR WAS pathetic. He was already playing out in his mind, the verbal abuse he would unleash on the car hire receptionist. The large sedan had gradually become more and more sluggish the further he drove it. Would nothing go right for him in this cursed country? He wound his way through block after block, hoping to catch a glimpse of Lydia or the redheaded friend. Mason had started at the northern end of town and systematically zig-zagged his way southward. He hoped Lydia had let her guard down, not expecting Mason to have caught up with her as quickly as he did. She never really grasped just how resourceful the man really was.

Mason stroked his beard angrily as he turned down yet another palm-tree laden street; one that looked exactly like the one before it and the one before that. He reached over, retrieved his phone from the passenger seat and scowled at his GPS; it was getting harder to keep track of the areas he had already covered. He began to veer over to the right side of the road, still not quite used to staying left. What was with this driving on the left crap anyway? The loud honk of another driver's horn cut through his consciousness, forcing him to hit the brakes and look away from his phone. A fast travelling vehicle swerved to miss him, still sounding the horn as it went past. Mason punched the steering wheel, once, twice, three-times, before throwing his phone against the passenger door.

Mason took a deep breath and he tried to focus on the task at hand. He took off slowly and kept scanning the houses and the sidewalks either side of the road. There were high-rise blocks of apartments and hotels on most streets, near the central business district, but the street he was on now featured the occasional house. Structures on stilts, made of wood and painted white. Mason saw the odd elderly person, pottering around in their front yards. Leaves were being raked, bushes watered and lawns mowed. An older woman meticulously tended to a shrub that sported bright, tropical flowers and Mason shook his head; what was the point? Dig all that garbage up and lay down some neat and tidy looking concrete; why create more work for yourself? Mason looked over the floral obligations in each yard; there were roses, some pink, cabbage-looking thing and irises, like the ones Lydia's mom used to yak about. Irises.

Mason turned the sub-standard sedan so hard, the tires screeched a little. He pulled up outside the large house and turned off the ignition. He hadn't seen irises in any of the other yards, not that he could remember. This was too easy wasn't it? Maybe it was fate. Looking around for signs of life, he found himself fidgeting and breathing heavily. Was he nervous? Enraged? What was it? Mason started the car up again; better to park on the other side of the street, he thought. After parking a couple of doors down. on the opposing side, Mason stepped out of the vehicle and, still looking around furtively, he crossed the road and approached the front gate. The dirt around the base of the flowers looked fresh enough; she had only recently arrived, it made sense. Mason opened the gate and walked in. He looked up at the street-facing windows; the shades were all drawn so he couldn't gage whether the occupant was home or not.

Mason thought for a moment about simply knocking; he could pass himself off as just another lost tourist if the wrong person answered. There was definitely someone home; there was a car in the driveway. If *she* answered, well, he'd make things up as he went along. Still, the element of surprise was on his side; better to bide his time and do it right. Mason opted to take the thin walkway up the side of the house to the backyard. He opened the side gate and crouched down behind an oleander bush so as not to be seen from the house or by anyone in the yard. He could see no one and so he scuttled over to a large eucalyptus tree in the center of the grass. Mason peered out from behind the tree and could see that all the shutters were closed on the windows at the rear, save for one. He watched for several minutes before a woman appeared.

Mason had to squint to see the woman properly. Her hair looked brown at first, but then the sun hit it, confirming it as ginger-colored. Was that Lydia's art store friend? Mason had to stare for a while, so long that he worried about being discovered. After straining to remember every detail he could of the woman he'd met so long ago, Mason finally had the very definite feeling that it was indeed Lydia's work-mate. "Gotcha' you bitch!" Mason whispered to himself. The woman pulled a patterned scarf off her head and shook her blazing red hair before re-tying it. She looked out into the yard and wondered where her friend might have got to. With any luck she'd made up with Dean and they were staring deeply into one another's eyes. Dora smiled and was about to leave when she saw something in the yard that made her blood run cold.

Mason knew, that even if he hadn't stumbled upon Lydia's home, he'd be able to squeeze this friend of hers for information; he'd enjoy it. He disappeared behind the tree and sat there, visualizing the things he'd do to red-hair to make her talk. He'd spotted an axe on his way in; that might help. There was every chance that Lydia was staying in the house too, so Mason decided on staking the place out, just to be sure. He sat behind the tree and waited; he was so close now. There was a sweet feeling of effervescence in his stomach; the feeling of excitement.

For at least twenty minutes, Mason kept watch. He listened for the sound of an engine starting, or the opening of the back door. Nothing. Had that witch seen him from the window? There was no way; he'd been careful and he was too far away for a little woman to spot him, with her little beady eyes. Mason considered storming the place; he could kick down that back-door without neighbors and passersby rubber-necking. He stroked his beard and stood up; the moment he'd been anticipating had come. Mason marched for the back door by way of the chopping block. He picked up the axe and was almost all the way there when he heard the noise of an engine. Was ginger-hippie leaving? No, this was the sound of a much larger car and it was definitely pulling in, not out. Mason tip-toed his way down the side passage for a look. He craned around the corner of the house and saw something that made his face drop: a man in uniform, stepping out of a police car.

Mason wasted no time; he ran as quietly as he could back down the side of the house and, after ditching the axe, vaulted over the side fence into the neighbor's yard. A scruffy looking dog started to bark and give chase. Mason bolted through the open driveway and out the front. Staying low, he skulked along the sidewalk toward his sedan. He could see the cop talking to red-hair at the front door; the conversation looked serious. The Police Officer looked around the front yard like a barn owl looking for mice. Mason had to practically dive behind a bush on the other side of the road, to avoid being seen. He wondered what Lydia had told her friend; had she shown red-hair a picture of him? Did she and the cop know what he looked like? He was wearing a cap and sunglasses, but would that be enough to put them off? Clearly the ginger-hippie had seen something when Mason was hiding out back, thus the cop at her door. Mason cursed the right hand-drive of his Australian hire-car, as he snuck around on the road-side to get in.

He hazarded another glance at the cop; he was being invited inside. Mason slunk down in his seat and checked the time on his phone. How long could their little visit really go on? The cop would see that there was no intruder and he'd chalk it all up to feminine paranoia, surely. Mason pulled out some trail mix that he'd stowed in the glove compartment and the hunting knife he'd bought that morning, fell onto the floor. Mason looked at the long blade in its camouflage sheath and smiled, before putting it away. He was a hunter; he would wait for his prey to arrive, or for red-hair to leave and lead him to her.

Mason had almost dozed off before the cop and red-hair emerged from the side of the house. He slid down in his seat and tentatively looked over the safety of the door and out through the faded tinting of the car window. He could see the policeman saying his goodbyes and heading for the car; thank the stars for that. Red-hair then closed and locked the door behind her as well. She bounded down the stairs; clearly too spooked to stay in the house alone. That was good; Mason wanted her to be afraid. Mason waited for the ginger-hippie to drive before starting up his own car. He then carefully tailed her, staying at least one car behind her once they hit the busier roads nearer town. They wove through the streets that approached the ocean until red-hair finally pulled up her aqua-blue hatchback on the main stretch of The Esplanade.

Mason swore as he saw Lydia's friend disappear amongst a crowd of people that were setting up stalls for some kind of beachside market. Mason parked a good distance away from the fracas, but close enough so that he could perform reconnaissance. Mason pulled a monocular from the pocket of his cargo shorts and watched intently. Eventually, the redhead appeared at her car from out of the crowd; opening it up and pulling out her own paraphernalia. She perched herself at a stall that had been set up by a tall man with dirty, blonde dreadlocks and a portly woman with rings in her face. Red-hair plonked a sign onto the long, shared table that read: Madame Dora: Psychic and Mystical Advisor Extraordinaire.

DEAN PULLED UP OUTSIDE the workshop and quickly made for the large, metal door. He opened the padlock and flew inside, Lydia following closely behind.

"This place should be pretty safe, while I get a few things" Dean said as he grabbed Lydia's shoulder-bag from her and kicked a wooden door at the back of the room. The door opened up to reveal a staircase, with another locked door at the top of it. The pair ran up the stairs and after opening the second door, they entered a small, sparsely furnished apartment.

"This was where you were going to move to?" Lydia asked, taking in the cramped surroundings.

"It's not as swish as my other place, but it's private," replied Dean defensively.

"I'm not saying it's a bad place. It's just that... you deserve better."

"We're going to have better. After we've put enough miles between us and your ex. We're going to live here," Dean said.

"Here?" Lydia questioned.

"Here," Dean clarified, pointing to several drawings of the exterior and interior of a house. The structure was spacious, with exposed rafters and wooden beams throughout.

"It's beautiful. There's so much... wood. It's really you," Lydia remarked.

"It's really *us*. If you like it, that is," Dean added.

"I love it!" exclaimed Lydia.

"And there's plenty of room for, you know, little bikers," said Dean almost shyly.

"Hey! Slow down there, soldier!" countered Lydia, laughing and smacking Dean's arm. She couldn't help but feel a shimmer of anticipation for what their life together could be.

"Okay, I'd better get busy. I've got enough stuff here; we won't need to go back to the big house. Won't be long."

Lydia wandered the apartment. She ran her fingers through the foliage of a potted philodendron and leafed through some motorbike magazines on the kitchen counter. In her hunt for more reading material, she pushed aside some thick books and discovered a stack of drawings. Some of the drawings looked like rough sketches of tables and bookcases, but amongst them was a drawing of a face: Lydia's face. It was a good sketch and it had a child-like idealism about it that gave Lydia butterflies. Lydia smiled to herself; she felt a deepening connection to Dean at that moment and she ran to find him. She found him in the tiny bedroom, still packing. As she entered, Dean looked up; he was gripping something, something angular and black.

"What the hell is that?" Lydia demanded, her warm feelings giving way to shock.

"An extra precaution. I'm not aiming to use it, if it can be avoided," Dean replied.

"Don't people who carry guns, usually end up getting shot?"

"We went to the range so you'd feel a little more comfortable around this thing, so you'd feel more confident," Dean offered.

"I thought it was to let off steam," Lydia countered.

"I just want all bases covered. If your ex catches up with us, who knows what he'll be packing."

"Not a gun. He hates guns. He's more of a bare-fists and prejudice kinda' guy. Besides, what if we get pulled up by the cops?"

"Look, if you really don't want me to take it, I won't," Dean said sincerely.

Lydia pictured Mason, his features twisted with rage and his bulk charging at Dean, the man she felt more for with each passing moment. She remembered the stark reality of the fresh bullet wound she and Dora had tended to for Dean and she couldn't bear the thought of him being hurt again. She knew that Dean would fight heart and soul for her; it was comforting and terrifying. She also knew that Mason's vengeance would be terrible.

"I trust you and I know you're not stupid. Promise me that you'll get rid of it once we're far enough away," Lydia pleaded.

"I promise," Dean said earnestly. Lydia believed him.

The pair rushed down the stairs and Dean quickly tied up their luggage in the tray of his utility vehicle. He covered up their things with a tarp and strapped it down tightly. He then parked his bike in the workshop and covered it; he took one last long look at his old life and closed the door on it for good.

"What about your things? What about all your beautiful work? The chair, Dean! We've left it at my place!" Lydia blurted in a panic.

"We'll contact Dora and I'll organize freight for everything we need. I'll even get them to pick up your flowers. To be honest, I'm sorta' looking forward to starting a new workshop, something bigger this time."

"Doesn't anything ever get you down, Dean Connors?"

"Not when you're with me," Dean replied.

"Oh, you're a big old corn-ball," Lydia replied laughing.

"Maybe. The thing is, Lydia: I mean it."

They hopped in the truck and looked at one another; this was it, they would be joined together by this experience always, no matter the outcome. Dean started the engine and they drove off; northbound, toward better things.

Chapter Seven

The Stand

Lydia tried to close her eyes and clear her mind, but the image of Dora's face kept appearing there. Mason had met her at least once at the art store, Dora had told her. Luckily Mason wasn't one for remembering her friends, or anything or anyone that loomed large in her life. The Gold Coast was a big place and he'd have a hell of a time searching for her. She'd kept a reasonably low profile; she hadn't really met anyone while she was there, apart from Officer Barnes and Dean of course. All evidence to the contrary, though, Lydia still felt like there were loose ends. She could feel a large, heavy stone sitting in her gut. How long would it take for that feeling to go away? Would it ever subside?

Dean reached across and squeezed Lydia's hand, as though he could sense what she was feeling.

"It's going to be okay," he yelled over the roar of the engine. Lydia smiled at him; there was something about Dean's voice that soothed her.

"You know, I can't argue with a man as good looking as you," Lydia said with a laugh.

"Righto," replied Dean, smiling. "You try to get some shut-eye. I'll wake you up later for something to eat."

Lydia didn't think she would be able to sleep, with all the stress and adrenaline of the day still taking its toll. But as soon as she closed her eyes and sunk back into her seat, she realized how exhausted she really was and the world went dark. Images rushed at her and in Lydia's frenetic dreamscape she saw Mason again. This time, however, he wasn't a giant or a monster but an ordinary man. He said nothing and did nothing; he just stood there, staring at Lydia with his blue eyes. Neither Dean nor Dora were there this time and Lydia felt an emptiness that scared her. Lydia's first instinct was to run, but then she felt something she had never really allowed herself to feel during her years with him: defiance. She approached the man without breaking eye contact, without playing with her sleeves or fidgeting. Lydia soon found herself running toward Mason, fueled by rage and resentment at the large portion of her life he had stolen. When she was nearly upon him, Lydia closed her eyes and brought her arm across her face and charged him like a football player. Mason wailed and shattered into countless pieces like a pane of glass; then there was nothing.

LYDIA AWOKE TO THE smell of meat cooking and Dean softly shaking her, "Come on, let's get fed," he said enthusiastically. Lydia blinked repeatedly until she could take in her surroundings. They were parked out the front of a roadside diner. There was a gas station on the far side and several large semi-trailers parked here and there. Lydia's stomach growled and she quickly closed and locked her door and ran to catch up with Dean, who was almost at the diner entrance.

Lydia and Dean wasted no time finding a booth and ordering food. The dishes were delivered speedily and there was little talk as the two hooked in to generous bowls of cheesy pasta. When Lydia had finished her serving, she looked around at the people in the diner. There were bus groups of tourists just passing through and families on driving holidays. In the corners, sat the occasional lost soul, avoiding eye-contact with everyone else. A young child screamed at being denied a second bowl of ice cream. An older couple chattered incessantly as they slowly worked through their small mountains of fruit salad. Two cops ambled in and Lydia looked down into her empty bowl, though she didn't know why. A paranoid voice told her that the police man and woman, now ordering coffee, knew about the gun Dean had brought with them. Lydia shot Dean a look and he just winked and grinned at her.

"Where are we?" Lydia asked, realizing that she had no idea.

"We're just past a place called Noosa. Famous for its beaches, water sports and curiously huge portions of spaghetti," Dean said, in a nasal news-anchor style voice.

"Well that sounds-" Lydia stopped and looked inside her handbag. She pulled her vibrating phone out and held it to her ear. Her face was suddenly ashen, her expression grim.

"What is it?" whispered Dean.

Lydia dropped the phone into her lap, "It's him. He has Dora."

MASON THREW DORA'S phone onto the floor of the living room; it smashed and bits scattered here and there. Dora's eyes streamed with tears as she struggled against her restraints. The cord that Mason had cut from Dora's venetian blinds, dug into her wrists. The chair that he had tied her to was an old, rickety one; maybe she could break it? But then what? Mason was a lot bigger and stronger than when she'd met him in America; it looked like he'd been training for this moment. Had he anticipated Lydia's escape? Even someone as broken as Mason must have known that Lydia was miserable. Dora pictured him as a tree, growing around Lydia and entrapping her; tightening his choke-hold over time and ultimately suffocating the woman he claimed to love.

"She's on the way. You better hope she's quick," Mason drawled without a hint of emotion.

He was aggressive, like a pit-bull tearing at a rabbit, when he'd followed Dora to her front door; he'd pushed her inside with such force, that Dora thought he intended to kill her. But then Mason had gradually chilled out; a look of Zen-like calm washing over him, as though he were completing some kind of military operation. That huge knife he'd held to Dora's neck felt so sharp, she worried that one slip of the wrist might sink it into her skin, like a fork into cheesecake.

"You don't have to do this!" Pleaded Dora.

"I don't have to do anything, that's true. But what's life without a little fun? Don't tell me you're not getting off on all this. You're probably moistening your seat with excitement," Mason said darkly.

"Lydia's a good person. She has a kind heart and she's more than you ever deserved. She doesn't need you anymore, she never did!"

Dora was careful not to use Mason's name; she had read that denying a thing its name, stripped it of power. She used to encourage Lydia to avoid naming her oppressor as well; not that it made much of a difference. Dora couldn't imagine how the man had found her. She felt unsettled by the thought of him tracking her, like a deer in the forest. How long had he watched her? What would he do to her; what would he do to her friend? Dora silently prayed to every entity she could think of, that Lydia wouldn't be hurt by this man yet again.

Mason kicked Dora, hard, in the shin, "Women are all the same. You all cling to each other like witches in a coven. You're the worst of all, probably. I bet you've poisoned her mind against me, silly cow," he blurted.

"You're the poisonous one, bucko! You're a tumor that needs to be cut from Lydia's life!"

Mason slapped Dora in the face and blood trickled from the corner of her mouth. She inhaled deeply, determined not to give him the satisfaction of upsetting her. She turned her head back toward him and stared into Mason's eyes; Mason glowered back for a moment and then looked away, huffing with frustration. He pointed his knife Dora's way threateningly, before thrusting it back into its sheath.

Mason paced up and down in front of Dora, whistling a tune. Dora tried to distract herself by trying to guess what the tune was. It sounded like Beethoven? Mozart maybe? Dora gave up eventually and focused on what she would do when Lydia arrived. Maybe she could distract Mason and give Lydia a chance to incapacitate him somehow. Dora hoped desperately that Lydia had called the police. She closed her eyes tightly and tried to silently communicate with Lydia; Dora had been working on mind expansion and telepathy for years, but the situation she now found herself in was so bleak, she found it hard to concentrate on anything but Mason's monstrous face.

DORA FELT DEHYDRATED and hazy when she heard the knock at the door; her legs were numb and her wrists hurt like hell. How long had it been? An hour, maybe two? Mason sprang upright; he'd been sitting on the sofa. Dora watched him disappear up the hallway and she listened keenly as the door was opened and some harsh, whispered words were exchanged. Mason's broad back came into view first; he was walking in reverse with his arms outstretched. Dean appeared and he seemed to be leading Mason into the living room.

"Drop the bloody knife!" Dean spat, pulling the slide back on his semi-automatic handgun.

"Who the hell are you?" Mason demanded.

"Never mind all that," Dean countered.

"Dora!" screamed Lydia, running over to embrace her friend. Lydia kissed Dora's face and then rounded the chair to start work on freeing her friend. There was a short, sharp bellow, followed by a scuffle. Lydia looked up to see that Mason had thrown himself at Dean, slamming him against the wall. Dean threw a barrage of punches at Mason's face, but the large man barely seemed to register pain. Dean brought a knee up to Mason's chest and attempted to push the man away from him. Mason barely budged; he repeatedly punched Dean in the ribs and stomach as Lydia and Dora screamed for him to stop. Mason turned to look at the women, before headbutting Dean; there was a sickening 'pop', followed by a torrent of blood spurting from Dean's nose. Dean dropped the gun and Mason dove for it.

"Now, you! Sit!" shouted Mason pointing the weapon at Dean, then at the sofa. He then indicated that Lydia should do the same. Still pointing at Lydia, then Dean and back again, Mason bent down and retrieved his hunting knife with his free hand. He tucked the sheathed knife into the waistband of his shorts.

"Let Dean and Dora go! This is just about you and me!" exclaimed Lydia.

"Oh no, no, no. This... is about all of us. 'Dean', huh? Nice name... for a douche-bag. You're the one that's been screwing my soul-mate? Was she good, Dean? Did she scream your name?"

"You're being disgusting!" Yelled Lydia.

"Me? I'm not the one fornicating my way through the Australian populace. And since when were you so confident? Talking back to Big Daddy like that? A fling or two and my lamb has become a fully- grown sheep!"

"What the hell is wrong with you?" Dean interjected.

"What business is it of yours, lover-boy? You think you're getting away with all this?"

"You make me sick, man. Man? Beating a woman, you're not a man at all, are you? You're a weak little coward."

Mason's eyes widened and he pulled his knife from its sheath. With one lightning fast motion, he slashed Dean's face. Lydia screamed and threw herself on Dean. Blood poured from the wound but Dean barely flinched; he just fixed his gaze on Mason, eyes boring into the man with contempt.

"Now, I did have a whole evening planned, but with the advent of our unexpected male consort here, things are going to have to take a whole different turn," oozed Mason.

"I've gotta' suggestion for you, fancy-man. How about you and I head into the yard and sort this out in the old way? No gun, no knife, just you and me," suggested Dean, with steely determination.

"Well aren't you brave. No, I've got a counter offer. Now, hear me out, compadre. I'm gonna' start by teaching my girl, Lydia, here about obedience and you're gonna' pay attention during the entire show. Then, to teach *you* about love and commitment, me and her are gonna' get down and dirty. You may even learn a thing or two, you little pissant. No one screws like me, hey buttercup? Then at the end, I may just give you the pleasure of having your head punched in by a real man. How 'bout that?"

"You mother f-" Dean began.

"No. There's no stopping him, Dean," interrupted Lydia, placing a hand on Dean's chest.

"But..."

"... trust me," Lydia added.

"See, man. She's been aching for the real thing all this time. Don't blame yourself, you haven't got what it takes to plough this treacherous little whore," said Mason.

Mason leant forward and took Lydia's hand. He yanked her up off the sofa and forcefully pulled her toward him. He then stared over Lydia's shoulder, squarely at Dean, as he ran his beefy hand down Lydia's back, to her buttocks. Mason then spun her around; he inserted the knife into one of the gaps between the buttons on the front of her dress. Dean made to lunge forward suddenly, but Lydia waved him away. Mason sliced one of Lydia's buttons clean off, then another.

Lydia broke away and just as Mason opened his mouth to protest, she dropped down onto her knees. Mason smiled at Dean as Lydia tugged at the zipper of his boardshorts. She felt around inside the opening and then, finding what she wanted, Lydia looked up at Mason seductively. Lydia licked her lips and sighed, flirtatiously. Dean winced uncomfortably, as she rubbed, stroked and massaged and Mason moaned. Lydia's efforts soon became more vigorous and Mason's eyes rolled into the back of his head. He then wrapped a hand around the back of Lydia's head and forced her face toward his crotch. Lydia then squeezed as hard as she could; Mason stepped back and let out a strained growl, but not before Lydia brought her other hand, clenched into a fist, toward his crotch at full velocity again and again. Mason squealed and doubled over in agony, loosening his grip on the gun. Lydia batted the weapon out of Mason's hand as Dean shot up from the sofa. He threw a rigid arm out over Mason's throat and pushed downward with all his strength. Mason hit the floor, the back of his head landing first with a sharp crack.

Dean felt Mason's neck for a pulse and looking up at Lydia, he nodded to indicate that their assailant was still alive. Dean grabbed Mason's knife and sprang over to Dora to cut her loose; he had only cut a couple of strands when he flew backwards onto the floor. Mason knelt over him, his face distorted with hatred. He stomped on Dean's face with a large, sneakered foot. His facial expression changed to one of bewilderment as he felt something knock him off balance. Dora had gotten free and propelled herself onto Mason's back. Grasping hold of his thick neck with one arm, she hammered his shoulder-blades with her free hand. Mason dropped to one knee, keeping his balance with a hand on the floor.

He suddenly stood up and threw himself and Dora against the wall. Dora let out a cry as she dropped off of Mason's back. Lydia rushed forward to help her friend, but Mason landed a powerful blow to her jaw, causing her to hit the ground. Mason picked Dora up by the scruff of the neck, like she weighed nothing. Dora's legs writhed as she tried desperately to get free, before going limp with exhaustion. Dora looked down at Lydia, her expression calm. Lydia watched through bleary eyes as Mason thrust his large, cruel knife into Dora's chest and belly again and again. The sound of metal piercing flesh, tearing muscle and grazing bone was sickening.

Mason carelessly dropped Dora's lifeless body on the carpet, his arm dripping with her blood. He smiled at Lydia as she brought her knees up to her chest and sobbed hysterically. Mason then turned his attention to Dean. He pinned Dean down and began punching him in the face. Mason's fists were soon both torn and bloody, as he rained blows on Dean. Mason looked tired, but determined, as he worked at killing the man that Lydia had chosen over him. Dean struggled less and less as the beating continued and Lydia shook violently with grief and rage.

Lydia felt around and gradually found her footing, "Get off him!" she screamed, rising to her feet and, pointing Dean's pistol at Mason's forehead.

"You won't do it, little lamb," Mason uttered groggily, as he began beating Dean again.

Lydia's arms shook, her legs trembled and her pulse quickened. Sweat streamed down over her brow and into her eyes. She felt both hot and cold at once and she thought for a moment that she might throw up. She wasn't going to shoot Mason; he was going to beat Dean to death, then he was going to kill her. Poor Dora didn't deserve her fate; neither her nor Dean should have been involved. She was stupid to try to escape; this was running away from home all over again. There was no escaping who she was. Lydia's arms slowly dropped; it was time to face up to what she really was: nothing.

Bang! Mason's eyes bulged and he let out a tortured groan; the bullet hole in his chest bled immediately and profusely. Mason couldn't believe that she had done it; she'd shot him. Mason looked up at Lydia incredulously. He crumpled as though all the air had escaped his body at once. The big man fell right on top of Dean. Lydia dropped the gun with a gasp; she knelt down and tugged at Mason's body. Dean summoned all his remaining strength and helped Lydia shift Mason's considerable weight. Awkwardly, she helped Dean up onto the sofa; then Lydia crouched next to Dora, trying in vain to revive her. She phoned the paramedics and then she called the only other person that she trusted to handle the situation.

Lydia tended to Dean as best she could; the two of them just sat for a time and stared back and forth at one another. The pair were silent, occasionally hazarding a glance at Dora's body on the living room floor and trying not to look at Mason. The paramedics banged on the door and Lydia sprung up to usher them in. They checked on Dora first and confirmed Lydia's fears: she was beyond saving. Her best friend was dead. They checked on Mason as Lydia bawled inconsolably; Mason was still alive but they said they'd have to move him fast. Lydia shuddered as Dean held her.

"Hello?" came a voice from the front of the house. Officer Barnes walked in, his hardened features giving way to shock, as he surveyed the scene in Dora's living room.

"Officer, meet my ex," Lydia said dryly, pointing at Mason who was now being hoisted into a stretcher.

"God almighty," said Officer Barnes, his gaze suddenly dropping to Dora's body in the middle of the room. The policeman looked up at Lydia and then Dean; a knowing expression on his weathered features.

"It was me, Officer. I shot the guy, right after he killed Dora," offered Dean, standing up and slowly approaching Officer Barnes.

"Look, son, I've told you before: I'm not stupid, Dean Connors, or should I call you Daniel? I followed up on that info you gave me about your old associates, valuable stuff. I've spoken to some trusted colleagues in the right departments and they're going to start the process of shutting that whole operation down. I also appreciate what poor Dora told me about the bastard now hurtling toward the hospital," Officer Barnes said calmly.

"The way I see it, Mason Wahl arrived alone and killed Dora and I got here just in time to take him down. You and your lady-friend, I've never seen before," Officer Barnes said looking at Dora's body.

"You for real?" Dean queried.

"What weapon was used to shoot the prick?" asked Officer Barnes.

"It's a Glock 17," answered Dean.

"Good. I won't have to stretch the truth too much on my report then. You'd best hand the firearm over to me, before you vanish. You got places you can disappear to for a while, I expect?"

"Yeah. We got somewhere," Dean added, looking back at Lydia.

"The wrong person died here tonight, Brian," Lydia said grimly.

"Well, way I see it, we're all made of the same matter in the end, forged in the furnaces of space," replied Officer Barnes, staring at Dora's body with glassy eyes.

"Sounds like something Dora would say," Lydia remarked.

"She did, in fact. Funny thing is, it was while I was trying to shut down an unauthorized, pop-up market in town that she was working at. She saw the world differently, Dora did. She was one in a million," Officer Barnes added, quickly wiping his nose and blinking repeatedly.

Two quick shadows bounded into the room, flattening out and sitting like sphinxes, before the body of their mistress.

"Boys! Can you take care of Romulus and Remus?" enquired Lydia.

"'Course I can," replied Officer Barnes.

Lydia stood and hugged the Policeman, "Thank you. For everything."

"You'd best make a move. Place will be crawling with uniforms before long. My partner... sees reason most of the time. Got him trained to wait in the car when the need arises, but I can only keep the powers back for a short time on this one. Go on, get," Officer Barnes commanded with the merest hint of warmth in his eye.

Epilogue

Dean pulled the truck up out the front of his sister's house. The structure sat high up on stilts and looked not unlike Lydia's rental on the Gold Coast. There were clumps of palm trees on either side of the front stairs and a gentle breeze made them sway idyllically. Lydia spilled out onto the grass that served as a sidewalk and breathed in the balmy, Far North Queensland air. The clouds were grey and moody and warm rain had started to fall in drips and drops as though the heavens couldn't decide either way. Dean rounded the vehicle and wrapped his rough hands around Lydia's waist. With one swift heave, he lifted her up onto the hood of the pickup. Lydia draped her forearms over Dean's shoulders.

"I'll never forgive myself for not going to Dora's funeral," she said.

"I think she would have understood. I mean that," Dean offered.

"Maybe you're right. I'll still always feel guilty and I'll always miss her."

"Of course, you will. You should. She was a good person. Too good for what happened. You didn't ask for any of this, though, Lydia. It's not your fault."

"I know but-"

"It's not your fault."

"Well, we made it," Lydia said, holding back her tears.

"Was there any doubt, 'Just Lydia'?" Dean asked.

"Wow. You remember that? Seems like a lifetime ago. How's your shoulder?"

"Just fine," Dean answered.

"And this?" Lydia asked as she gently ran the back of her hand across the freshly stitched knife-wound on Dean's cheek. She touched her fingertip to the other cuts and abrasions on his face, like she was taking an inventory.

"Ow! Okay, some of those hurt," Dean chuckled.

"I was so scared."

"We're here together now. That's all I want to think about," Dean countered.

"Officer Barnes texted me to say that Mason would be going to court as soon as he could arrange it. It should be him in the ground," Lydia's protest was cut off midway by Dean planting his lips on hers. Dean drew back and brushed some stray hairs off of Lydia's forehead.

"I love you, Lydia Hawkins," Dean said earnestly.

"Oh, come on," Lydia said.

"I. Love. You." said Dean firmly, followed by Lydia's favorite, easy smile. Lydia hugged Dean tightly.

"I love you too, Dean Connors."

Don't miss out!

Visit the website below and you can sign up to receive emails whenever Kira Parke publishes a new book. There's no charge and no obligation.

https://books2read.com/r/B-A-KFEH-VTMW

BOOKS2READ

Connecting independent readers to independent writers.

---

1. https://books2read.com/u/4jDVvk

2. https://books2read.com/u/4jDVvk

Also by Kira Parke

Tropic Storm
Protected
Cyclone

Standalone
The Goddess of the Sea
They Never Came Back
Envious Green

9 798230 496021